Isabelle
then a figure below.

It was a man and he was intentionally pulling her under.

He reached for her arm and yanked her lower, then grabbed her head and pushed her down, too strong for her to fight against, but that didn't stop her from trying. She kicked and flailed at the figure. Finally, she managed to push to the surface, gasping for air the moment she broke through the waterline.

"Help me," she cried as the strong hands pulled her under once more.

Then there was splashing in the water and moments later the man released her. She surfaced again and struggled to catch her breath and tread water, coughing and gasping as she did so until another pair of strong hands grabbed her and she flinched.

"It's okay. I've got you." The voice was husky and weighted with worry, but she knew it instantly.

Drake.

At that moment, it didn't matter whether or not he was her deceased husband. All that mattered was that he was there for her.

Virginia Vaughan is a born-and-raised Mississippi girl. She is blessed to come from a large Southern family, and her fondest memories include listening to stories recounted around the dinner table. She was a lover of books from a young age, devouring tales of romance, danger and love. She soon started writing them herself. You can connect with Virginia through her website, virginiavaughanonline.com, or through the publisher.

Books by Virginia Vaughan

Love Inspired Suspense

Lone Star Defenders

Dangerous Christmas Investigation
Missing in Texas
Protecting the Texas Witness

Cowboy Protectors

Kidnapped in Texas
Texas Ranch Target
Dangerous Texas Hideout
Texas Ranch Cold Case

Cowboy Lawmen

Texas Twin Abduction
Texas Holiday Hideout
Texas Target Standoff
Texas Baby Cover-Up
Texas Killer Connection
Texas Buried Secrets

Visit the Author Profile page at LoveInspired.com for more titles.

PROTECTING THE TEXAS WITNESS

VIRGINIA VAUGHAN

LOVE INSPIRED SUSPENSE
INSPIRATIONAL ROMANCE

LOVE INSPIRED® SUSPENSE
INSPIRATIONAL ROMANCE

Recycling programs
for this product may
not exist in your area.

ISBN-13: 978-1-335-95725-2

Protecting the Texas Witness

Love Inspired
22 Adelaide St. West, 41st Floor
Toronto, Ontario M5H 4E3, Canada
www.LoveInspired.com

Printed in Lithuania

MIX
Paper | Supporting
responsible forestry
FSC® C021394

And I will restore to you the years that the locust hath eaten, the cankerworm, and the caterpiller, and the palmerworm, my great army which I sent among you.
—*Joel* 2:25

This book is dedicated to all the dreamers.
If God has placed something in your heart,
never doubt He will bring it to fruition.

ONE

Isabelle Morris breathed a sigh of relief as she turned her SUV onto Mercy Highway. They'd made it to the Texas town of Mercy after driving all night, stopping only for gas and to rest for a few hours. Not that she'd really been able to sleep. She'd spent weeks feeling like she had to constantly look over her shoulder, and she knew she wouldn't really feel secure until they reached their destination—the quiet, peaceful lakeside cabin where no one knew to look for them. The place where she and her fifteen-year-old daughter would finally feel safe.

They'd been the recipients of a constant stream of threats and harassment over the past few weeks, ever since word had leaked that she'd be testifying in the fraud and embezzlement case against her former boss, Charles Jeffries. She'd endured it as best she could, but after her daughter had been confronted at the gym, Isabelle had had enough. She'd needed to get Kelsey away from that chaos for a while.

The cabin would be the perfect getaway. Hardly anyone even knew she had it. It had been her late husband's, inherited through his family, and she'd only ever been there a handful of times, preferring to rent it out for extra income. Kelsey, for her part, had never been there before.

They made it to the cabin with no problem. As Isabelle parked, Kelsey, who had been quiet and sullen for most of the drive, perked up at the sight of the lake. She jumped from the SUV and started to run down to the bank.

While her daughter shared more of her features than her father's, with her long blonde hair, thin build and green eyes, her attitude reminded Isabelle of Rayland every day. Friendly and outgoing, Kelsey was always looking for the next fun thing to do and jumping into it with both feet. Like Rayland, Isabelle often had to be the one to bring Kelsey back down to earth. Life couldn't always be fun. Isabelle called her back. "Let's unload and settle in first. Then you can explore."

Kelsey's shoulders drooped with disappointment, but she did as instructed and grabbed two suitcases and her duffel from the back of the car while Isabelle carried the remaining bags along with a box of food she'd grabbed before they'd left home. It wasn't much, but the decision to head to the cabin had been a spur of the moment one and food and supplies hadn't been high on her list of priorities. Not after the attack on Kelsey. She'd decided to get out of town fast under the cover of darkness before anyone with a shred of connection to Global Health or the Jeffries case knew she was gone.

She unlocked the front door to the cabin, disarmed the security system, then stepped inside. Kelsey's eyes grew wide, and she dropped the bags near the door as she surveyed the interior.

The cabin was large and spacious, with a living area with vaulted ceilings, a prominent fireplace and large panels of curtains covering windows that looked out onto the lake. It was clean and looked well cared for which she was glad to see. The last tenants had been here for over a year and had obviously cared for the place. Isabelle pushed the button that opened the curtains spanning the big glass doors that opened out to the lake. It was a beautiful scene.

"Wow," Kelsey commented as she glanced around. "This place is amazing. What's upstairs?" She darted up the stairs to check out the second floor without waiting for an answer.

Isabelle let her go. She was suddenly overwhelmed with thoughts of Rayland in a way that only happened when she was here. He'd loved this cabin and this town, where his grandparents had lived. He'd spent his summers here growing up and had wanted to pass on the love of Mercy to Kelsey, but he had died ten years ago, before he'd gotten the chance.

Rayland, I wish you were here now to help us through this.

Kelsey bounded back down the steps. Her eyes were wide with surprise and glee. "Can we swim in the lake?"

"Yes, we can. But first we have to get settled in. Take your bag upstairs and pick a room."

Kelsey did as she was told, lifting her duffel bag over her shoulder and heading back up the stairs. She hoped they could find some solitude here and take a breather from the constant turmoil that had become their everyday lives.

She hadn't anticipated how much being here reminded her of all the things she and Rayland had never gotten to do. This cabin should have been a place of fun for them but now it had become a hideout instead.

They unpacked, then Kelsey wanted to walk down by the lake, begging to be allowed to go by herself when Isabelle said she was too tired to join her. Eventually, Isabelle agreed. She sat on the outside deck and watched as Kelsey strolled down a path then disappeared from view behind a cluster of brush. She felt a burst of anxiety, but Isabelle took a deep breath and reminded herself that they were safe here. No one knew where they were so it was fine for Kelsey to be out of her sight for a few minutes.

She forced herself to go back inside and decided to make lunch in order to keep her mind off her daughter. She had only the necessities she'd brought from home along with a few items they'd picked up at stops along the way. They would have to make a grocery run later.

Isabelle mixed up some tuna for sandwiches then placed it into the refrigerator to keep fresh until Kelsey returned. She headed upstairs to wash and change clothes. She slipped into a pair of lounge pants and flip-flops and was relieved when she heard movement downstairs that must be Kelsey returning. However, when she heard the sound of glass breaking, she froze.

Kelsey wouldn't do that. Was it an intruder? She ran from the bedroom and glanced over the banister railing. A dark figure was moving through the cabin.

She pressed herself against the wall to hide then darted back into the bedroom and locked the door. Fear pulsed through her—not for herself but for her daughter. Kelsey might walk back into the cabin any minute to find an intruder.

She grabbed the phone and dialed Kelsey's phone number but the call went unanswered. She didn't even know if the girl had her phone with her. She'd emphasized the need not to call her friends and tell them where they were but she had stopped short of taking Kelsey's phone from her. Now she was glad she hadn't, but it didn't do any good if she wasn't answering it. When she couldn't reach Kelsey she called the sheriff's office.

The dispatcher answered quickly. "911, what's your emergency?"

"Someone's in my house. They're downstairs." She rattled off the address of the cabin.

"I'm dispatching someone to your house now," the woman explained. "What's your name?"

"Isabelle Morris. My daughter and I just arrived in town. She's down by the lake and I can't reach her. She's only fifteen. Please, I'm so afraid she's going to walk in on the intruder."

"Deputies are on the way, ma'am. Just stay in your room until they get there."

She heard a door close and feared the worst. Had Kelsey returned? "I think my daughter just came back. I have to go."

She heard the dispatcher say something about staying where she was, but Isabelle ignored the woman as she ended the call. Staying put wasn't a possibility, not with her daughter's life at stake. She spotted a toolbox in the corner of the closet and dug through it, pulling out a hammer to use as a weapon. She inched open the door and peeked out. She hadn't heard Kelsey's voice yet but she was certain she'd heard the door open and close. She crossed the hall and peeked into Kelsey's room. The girl wasn't there. Isabelle crept down the stairs, glancing left and right for the intruder and for her daughter. She didn't see either one, so she hurried toward the kitchen. Perhaps the intruder had left and that had been the door closing she'd heard. If that was the case, she would be very embarrassed when the sheriff's office deputies arrived. Oh well, she could deal with a little embarrassment. After what she'd been through the past few months, it was no wonder she was a little jumpy.

She spotted a broken window by the front door. Glass was on the floor. She gripped the hammer tighter. That had to be how he'd gotten inside. She hurried toward the kitchen and glanced through the windows and down by the lake. She saw no one, not even Kelsey.

Suddenly, someone grabbed her from behind and clamped their hand over her mouth. She tried to scream but the sound was muffled. Her assailant was stronger than she and did his best to pull her to the floor. Panic filled her and she used the hammer to batter at him.

She heard him cry out but his hold on her didn't loosen. She didn't let up on her attack, though. If he thought he was going to kill her, he was going to have a fight on his hands.

He slapped her hard, sending her tumbling to the floor. The hammer slipped from her grip and bounced across the tiled floor. She turned and confronted the man. He wore a ski mask covering his face but he pressed a hand to her neck, choking her. She kicked and struggled, doing everything she could to pull him off her, but it was no use. He easily overpowered her. In desperation, she clawed his mask with her fingernails, and he cried out and hit her again then pulled out a knife.

This was it. He was going to kill her and shut her up once and for all. Charles was finally going to get what he wanted—her off the case.

Suddenly the door burst open and four people in uniform rushed inside, guns raised. "Freeze," one of them commanded, and she realized it was the deputies arriving.

Her assailant leaped to his feet and took off out the patio door.

"Don't let him get away," one of them commanded.

Three of the deputies hurried outside after him. Isabelle sat up and grasped her throat where the man had held her. Her heart was racing but relief was beginning to settle her frantic nerves. She'd made it through the attack.

The remaining deputy holstered his gun and hurried to her, kneeling beside her. "Ma'am, are you okay? Did he hurt you?"

"I'm…a little bruised, I think. But nothing worse than that," she assured him.

"Maybe we should get you checked out just to be sure." His voice was soothing, comforting, as he radioed for an ambulance then came back to her. "Can you stand?"

He held out his hand, and she nodded and reached for it. Only then did she bother looking at him. She was nearly to her feet when she glanced up at him. That face… It wasn't a perfect match, but she couldn't help but recognize those piercing blue eyes. That prominent brow.

Her knees buckled and her head swam.

Impossible!

She lost her balance, and only the deputy's strong arms around her prevented her from hitting the floor again.

"Whoa, I've got you," he assured her, his mouth turning up into the one-sided grin she knew so well while his kind eyes shined down at her.

She couldn't believe her own eyes for a moment and wondered briefly if her attacker had knocked her out and she was hallucinating. What other way was there to explain what she was seeing? Only his strong embrace and the pain still radiating through her from the attack told her she was 100 percent awake.

Her eyes roamed the man's face and his outline. She reached out to touch strong arms and a firm chest. It was him. It was really him.

Her dead husband was alive and standing in front of her.

"Rayland!" She threw her arms around him and pressed herself against him.

Deputy Drake Shaw was used to people being appreciative of law enforcement showing up to help, but he'd rarely had such a beautiful woman throw her arms around him.

She could hardly stand, so he led the lovely blonde to the couch and had her sit. She seemed dazed and confused. What had she called him? Rayland? She looked ready to faint, so he did his best to keep her conscious. It was possible she'd hit her head or the intruder had drugged her before they'd arrived.

He picked up his radio. "Can I get an ETA on the ambulance?"

"Three minutes out," came the reply from dispatch. Good. This lady looked like she needed it. Her face had paled and she continued to stare at him with wide green eyes that rapidly filled with tears.

"Ma'am, are you okay? Can you talk to me?"

In response, she reached out to touch his cheek, surprising him and sending sparks against his skin. He'd never had that reaction before either.

"Rayland?"

She was calling him that name again. He didn't recognize it. Nor did he know her. Yet it wasn't impossible that they'd met before and he didn't remember her. An accident years earlier had caused him to suffer memory loss. However, he knew his name and it wasn't Rayland.

He touched her hand and gently moved it from his face. "My name is Deputy Drake Shaw of the Mercy County Sheriff's Office. Can you tell me yours?"

That only confused her more. She frowned. "Drake Shaw?"

He was going to have to make sure the EMTs checked her for head trauma.

Suddenly, a figure arrived at the door and darted inside. "Mama!" The girl looked to be around fourteen or fifteen and was a mini-me of the woman. She darted into the house and threw herself into the woman's arms. "What happened? Are you okay?"

That seemed to bring her out of her reverie. She pulled the girl into a hug. "I'm fine, sweetie. I'm okay." She grabbed the girl's face. "Are you okay? Are you hurt?"

"I'm fine. Why are the police here, Mom?"

She looked hesitant to answer but must have known she had to. "Someone broke in, Kelsey. He attacked me. Thankfully, the deputies arrived and ran him off."

Kelsey's chin quivered as she fought back tears. "Did they catch him?" She turned to look at Drake and repeated her question. "Did you catch him?"

"My people have gone after him. They're still searching." But since he hadn't gotten a notice over the radio that they'd found the intruder yet, it was likely the man had gotten away from them. He'd probably darted back into the woods before they could stop him. "Don't worry. We will find him."

Kelsey looked back at her mother. "Mom, does this mean we have to leave again?"

Instead of answering, she pulled the girl back to her.

Drake hadn't missed that "again" and it sent his radar up. Were these two on the run or hiding out from something? Anyone would be frightened from a break-in, but the girl's reaction told him they were already on guard even before this had happened.

He glanced at them both. Fresh, faint bruises were beginning to appear on the woman's fair skin, but the girl, Kelsey, had older bruises on her upper arm. It looked to him like the kind of bruise one got from being grabbed.

He looked back at the woman, who was still staring at him. "Can you tell me your name?" he asked her again.

"My name?"

Kelsey answered instead. "Her name is Isabelle Morris. You know that, don't you, Mom?"

Isabelle nodded. She seemed to recognize her daughter and her own name but something had her spooked, and he was glad when he heard the ambulance arrive on the scene. She hadn't stopped looking at him with a confusion he didn't understand. And why was she calling him Rayland?

He moved away so the paramedics could examine her. He radioed the deputies who'd arrived with him. "Have you found anything?" he asked them.

"Negative," Deputy Horner told him. "The suspect got away. Should we start a search of the area?"

"No, report back to the cabin to regroup. We'll see if we can find any forensic evidence." The man had worn a mask, but they should still be able to record his prints, and there was a chance they'd be able to gather fibers or blood evidence. He saw a discarded hammer on the kitchen floor—it seemed likely the woman had used it to defend herself. If it had struck the attacker, it might have picked up DNA evidence.

He phoned dispatch and asked Allison Meeks, the dispatcher on duty, to replay the 911 call for him. He'd listened to it as they'd approached the cabin and recalled that Isabelle had said they'd just arrived in town. He listened to the replay and heard it again. He needed to verify that statement but, if it was true, he had an idea who their intruder might have been.

He glanced back at Isabelle Morris and her daughter on the couch and found her gaze locked on him again. He figured it was as good a time as any to ask her questions, since she seemed to be out of her funk and was speaking coherently with the EMTs.

One of them stood and addressed him. "There doesn't appear to be any serious injury. She denies hitting her head or losing consciousness. I think she's mostly just shaken up. She's refusing to go to the hospital for further evaluation."

He thanked him then approached the two women again as the EMTs gathered their things and left. He slid into a chair facing them. "Do you feel up to answering a few questions now?" he asked Isabelle.

She nodded but turned to her daughter first. "Kelsey, would you fix me some tea?"

Kelsey agreed then got up and went into the kitchen. Once she was gone, Isabelle leaned forward to him. She stared at him then reached out to touch his face again, her hand warm against his skin. He was suddenly conscious of the scars on his skin.

She still looked confused, and it was obvious from her expression that she thought he was someone else. What had she called him earlier? He softened his tone. "I think you have me confused with someone else, ma'am. As I told you before, my name is Deputy Drake Shaw, not Rayland."

Tears formed in her eyes as they scoured his face.

"Who do you think I am?" he asked her.

She leaned back as her initial shock and disbelief seemed to give way to reality. "My husband. You remind me very much of my late husband, but you can't be him, can you?"

Understanding dawned on him. "I'm very sorry for your loss. How long has he been gone?"

Kelsey returned with a cup of tea, and Isabelle took it. Her hands shook as she lifted the cup to her lips then sipped before answering him. "Ten years. He died in an accident."

Now it was Kelsey's turn to look at him confused. "Are you talking about Daddy? What does he have to do with anything?"

Isabelle took her daughter's arm. "Nothing, sweetie. Nothing."

He did some quick math and realized Kelsey would have been very young when her father was killed. If he did indeed look like her late father, the girl might have been too young to realize it, and Drake's injuries could counteract any similarities to his photographs. He thought about asking more questions, but Kelsey was right to say that his resemblance wasn't what mattered here.

"I understand you two just arrived in Mercy? That's what you told the 911 operator."

She took another sip of her tea then nodded. "Yes, just this morning, in fact. This cabin belonged to my late husband's family. We've been renting it out for years, but it was empty so we thought we would come here and spend some time on the lake."

The girl cast her mom another confused look. He could see there was something more going on than they were letting on, but it might have nothing to do with the attacker, especially if, as he suspected, this break-in and attack was nothing more than an opportunistic occurrence.

"You say the cabin's been empty recently?"

"Yes, the last tenants moved out two months ago."

That seemed to fit Benny's modus operandi. "There's a man who lives in the woods a few miles from here. He's had some mental health issues and he's been known to break into empty cabins to scrounge for food and provisions. If, as you say, this place has been empty for a while, it's possible he didn't realize anyone was here."

"So you think he came here looking for food?" Kelsey asked.

He nodded. "It's possible." The ski mask he'd noticed the attacker wearing seemed an odd detail, especially given it was the heart of summer, but Benny could have been using it to make certain he wasn't identified entering cabins. "If it was him, now that he knows you're here, I doubt he'll be back. He's leery of confronting people."

Isabelle touched her neck. "He didn't seem very leery to me."

He didn't say it but the attack on her was odd for exactly that reason. "He's never been violent before. Your attacker disappeared into the woods, but I have an idea where Benny camps out. I'll go talk to him and see if there's any evidence of him being here." He watched them both and felt something was off. The bruises on the daughter plus the guarded behavior sent his antennas up. "Unless there's someone else you think could be responsible for this break-in? Someone who followed you here?"

Isabelle gave a firm shake of her head. "No. No one followed us here." She seemed to get her bearings back and turned to her daughter. "Kelsey, I made some tuna for lunch. It's in the refrigerator. Why don't you go eat. I'm going to sweep up this glass then I'll join you."

The girl did as she was told and walked out of the room.

"Would you like some help with that?" Drake asked her.

"No, I'll take care of it."

He noticed the busted window and zeroed in on that as the point of entry. "My team is going to be dusting for prints and looking around for other evidence. We won't take long. I can board that up for you afterward if you'd like."

"I would appreciate that," Isabelle stated.

Drake stood to take care of the task and spotted an alarm system by the front door. "Does this work?"

She stood at his question and nodded. "Yes. It was set when we got here but I didn't rearm it since Kelsey was outside."

"For the time being, you and your daughter might want to keep it on. I'm sure it won't be necessary again, but better safe than sorry, right?"

He went outside and spotted his team returning. They could dust for prints themselves without calling in a forensics team, but he also made sure to have them look for blood evidence. The assailant had had a knife when Drake entered the cabin...also atypical behavior for Benny, but their presence could have spooked him enough to lash out. If Benny had become violent, confronting him alone wouldn't be wise. Drake would have another deputy go with him.

"And search around the cabin as well," he commanded them. "Maybe he dropped the knife or something else as he fled."

His team got to work and so did he. He found nails and boards in a nearby shed then used them to cover the window. He made a note to phone the local glass shop in town to replace the pane. It was the least he felt he could do given their negative initial reception to town. It wasn't the way he liked to think of Mercy being represented. He loved this place and its people. It was a wonderful place to live, and according to Isabelle, although she'd owned the cabin for years, this was her first real time staying in the area. And this was her welcome—a break-in and assault. That wasn't acceptable.

He felt eyes on him as he worked and turned to see Isabelle standing in the doorway, her arms folded as she watched him. Still shaken up at the break-in? Or was she more rattled from seeing who she thought was her dead husband come back to life?

Something about her struck him as familiar and he wondered again briefly if they'd met before his accident. Doubtful. He might not remember a lot, but if their paths had crossed, she'd know him by his real name. He certainly couldn't be her husband. Not when he had his own family who remembered him. Those years were now a blank to him, but that wasn't the case for his sister or his deceased mother, both of whom had helped him recuperate after the accident. "I'm not him, you know," he reminded her. Part of him briefly wished he was. The lady was gorgeous even under the threat of an attack, and he liked how protective she was with her daughter.

She shook her head and closed her eyes. "I'm sorry. I'm making you uncomfortable. You're right. You can't possibly be Rayland. He's dead." She took a step toward him and held out her hand. "Thank you for your help, Deputy Shaw."

He took her hand to shake. "You're welcome, Mrs. Morris."

"Please, call me Isabelle."

"Isabelle. That's a beautiful name, by the way."

Her cheeks reddened at the compliment. "Thank you. I was named after my grandmother. Rayland and I named Kelsey after his grandmother."

"She looks like a good kid. Is she your only child?"

"Yes. She was only five when her father died. She doesn't have a lot of memories of him."

Since she was being so open about her life, he decided to ask her about his suspicions. "I couldn't help noticing the old bruises on Kelsey's arms. Are you and your daughter running from something or someone?"

She looked surprised by his question then gave him a placating smile. "We just needed to get away for a while, that's all. As I said, thank you for your help." She walked to the door and closed it, and he heard the locks engage.

So much for her hospitality. That was a clear sign that she was done with him.

TWO

As his team packed up and readied to leave, Drake asked Deputy Steve Gordon to come with him to find and question Benny. He agreed, so Drake radioed to dispatch that he'd finished up at the cabin and outlined their plan to confront him.

Benny McCarthy was a thirty-year-old man who'd suffered brain damage as a teenager after flipping his ATV. His mental state had continued to deteriorate ever since. He'd been in and out of treatment centers but nothing had seemed to help him. A few years earlier, he'd moved out of his mother's house and refused to return, choosing instead to camp out in the woods. He'd isolated himself, rarely speaking to anyone, but the sheriff's office had had several encounters with him after he'd been caught breaking into empty cabins and stealing from the owners. Only, like Drake had told Isabelle and her daughter, Benny usually targeted empty homes and, to Drake's knowledge, he'd never been violent. At least, not so far. It was possible that his mental state had deteriorated further. And if so, that needed checking into.

He drove to the mobile home owned by Mary McCarthy, Benny's mother. Mary answered and her face fell at seeing Drake. "The only time the police come is when Benny has done something wrong. What is it now?" she asked him, her hand on her hip.

"There was a break-in at a cabin. Mary, a woman was attacked."

She shook her head. "No, it couldn't have been him. My Benny's never been violent before."

"I know that. It's possible she startled him. They just moved in—Benny likely expected the place to be empty. I only want to talk to him. Do you know where he's at?"

She nodded. "That last time I saw him was a week ago. He was camped out by that tall oak tree a half mile south. Are you going to arrest him?"

"If I find evidence that he was involved, that he attacked this woman, I'll have no choice."

She nodded and stepped out onto her porch, closing the door. "I'll wait here for you."

Gordon and Drake drove as far as they could before the terrain became too rough for his SUV. From there, they walked.

He spotted the old oak tree Mary had indicated but didn't see anyone. As he approached, he scanned the area. He saw stuff lying on the ground—cans of food, blankets, matches—but nothing that looked like it had been taken from the cabin. It was possible Benny hadn't had time to rummage through the cabinets before Isabelle had confronted him. If so, that would make tying him to the break-in difficult.

Calling for him would do no good. It would simply send him running for cover. Gordon had moved away from the campsite in the direction of Isabelle's cabin, which was less than two miles away.

"Drake, come see this," he called.

Drake hurried to him. Along a path of trampled grass lay a black ski mask. He knelt and examined it. It matched the one the intruder had been wearing when Drake came through the door. He noticed a hole in the cheek area. It was too far away from Benny's campsite to automatically assume it belonged to him but it was suspicious. He retrieved a pair of gloves and an evidence bag and sealed the mask into evidence.

"This doesn't look good for Benny," Gordon commented.

"No, it doesn't," Drake admitted. "Let's spread out and search the area. Maybe he's hiding from us. And, remember, if he really is the man from the cabin, he has a knife on him."

They spent the next hour searching without finding Benny. Finally, they called it quits. They would have to come back later to find Benny. In the meantime, he would issue a county-wide BOLO for him.

He and Gordon walked to his SUV then headed toward the trailer where Mary was still waiting. "We didn't see him," Drake told her. "We'll come back."

"I have a hard time believing my Benny would attack a woman," she said.

He understood a mother defending her son—who wouldn't—but Benny had always been unpredictable. "I still have to speak with him," he told her. He held out the evidence bag holding the black ski mask. "Do you recognize this? Have you seen him with it?"

She glanced at it then shook her head. "No. Why would he need a hat like that? It's nearly a hundred degrees out."

Drake could only shrug. There was a lot they didn't have answers to yet.

Mary stood and sighed. "If he comes by, I'll try to convince him to come to the sheriff's office with me or else I'll call you."

"Call us, Mary."

He didn't envy the position she was in. She hadn't asked to have a son with this condition. On the other hand, he still needed to do his job, especially when a woman had been assaulted. Also, he knew Mary understood the need to have her son brought in and re-evaluated if he'd become violent.

He and Gordon headed to the sheriff's office. He needed to file his report on the break-in and his attempt to interview Benny. He also wanted to do a background check on Isabelle. Something just wasn't adding up with her. Back at his desk, he typed in Isabelle's information. Her criminal record came back clean but a quick Google search brought up links to her professional profile and some images of community service events.

Her last listed job had been at Global Health Systems. Drake had seen news reports about the embezzlement and fraud. When the scandal broke, public confidence in the company tanked, and it was soon forced to declare bankruptcy and shut its doors, putting hundreds of people out of work. Not to mention all the people who took a hit to their retirement savings when stock in the company became worthless.

Losing her job had to have been devastating for a single mom like Isabelle, but that was no reason for her to be in danger. Something more was going on here, even if he couldn't figure out what. He turned back to typing up his reports when Josh Knight, another deputy and the head of their tactical unit, plopped a report onto his desk.

"I was walking by the lab and they asked me to give this to you. It's fingerprint analysis on your intruder."

Drake opened the report only to find the prints they'd collected were inconclusive for matches.

"Benny's prints are in the system," Josh reminded him. "Does that mean he wasn't involved?"

"I'm not sure," Drake told him. "The guy was wearing a ski mask. It's possible he was also wearing gloves. I can't say I noticed. Either way, I still want to speak to him." He told him about the ski mask, now in forensics. "Gordon and I found it when we were out searching for him."

"Why would Benny wear a mask?"

"I don't know. We did find it near his camp, but he might not even have anything to do with this, Josh. The more I think on it, the less inclined I am to believe he was involved. We'll know more once we find and question him."

"What about the woman who was assaulted?"

"The victim and her daughter stated that no one from where they came from knows they're here." Which wasn't exactly the same as saying that there was no one from back home who might want to harm them. But a quick background check on Isabelle hadn't returned any red flags either. If she was hiding out, it wasn't from the law. Maybe she was right, and their attacker was a purely local problem.

"So it's possible there's a new burglar operating in the area, one that doesn't care if their targets are occupied and isn't afraid to use force."

That was the next logical conclusion. "Maybe so."

They both seemed to understand what that meant for the area. "I'll let the sheriff know about this then send the patrol unit an alert to be on the lookout for any suspicious activity in that area."

Drake finished up his report then submitted it. He decided to call it a night after a long, eventful day. His shift had officially ended three hours ago, but it wasn't unusual for him to work past it when handling the details of a case. Like many small towns, Mercy had its share of crime, mostly drug related, and criminal investigations didn't often fit into an official time frame. Some of his cases weren't urgent enough to mandate the additional hours, but he enjoyed the work and didn't mind if they did.

"Have a good night, Drake," Allison called to him as he waved to her then exited the building, climbed into his sheriff's office issued SUV and headed home.

He'd purchased a house two years ago. By that point, he'd been working at the sheriff's office for a few years and was finally feeling like he was settling down in Mercy. But from the time he'd first arrived, something about this town had drawn him in. He loved this place. He'd spent years roaming the country and looking for somewhere that appealed to him. It wasn't until he'd arrived in Mercy that he'd felt at home and decided to stay.

He walked into his house and plugged his cell phone into its charger, only then realizing he had a missed call from his sister. He hit the voicemail button and put it on speaker mode as the message played while he poured himself a tall glass of milk.

"Hey, Drake, it's Connie. I was just checking in with you, little brother. It's been a while since we've spoken. I miss you. Call me soon."

Her tone told him she was feeling lonely, and yet, instead of rushing to comfort her, he mostly felt reluctant to call her back. He loved Connie but his relationship with his sister was complicated. She hadn't approved when he'd left home after their mom's death six years earlier. He'd even tried to talk her into traveling with him, but roaming aimlessly from town to town and working odd jobs for food and gas hadn't been the life for her any more than working the small family farm had been for him. He'd accepted her decision—but she hadn't been as willing to accept his, telling him over and over again how betrayed she felt at the idea that he was leaving her all alone there.

She'd never married, having spent her life dedicated to caring for her family. She'd been the one to nurse Drake back to health after the accident had left him badly injured with no memory, all the while being a full-time caregiver for their cancer-stricken mother. He appreciated what she'd done…but gratitude on its own wasn't enough to tie him down to a place where he wasn't happy. Ever since the accident, Drake hadn't felt he'd belonged there. He'd had his own life to live, and he wished Connie would stop resenting him for it. But instead of being happy for him that he'd found a place where he belonged, or proud of him for becoming a deputy, their phone calls were mostly filled with her trying to guilt him into moving back. They'd been having the same argument for years, and he didn't want to have it again. The sad truth was, the "home" she wanted him to return to didn't feel like home to him at all. Not the way Mercy did. His hometown in Alabama was not a place he associated with good memories. If they'd had some once, he no longer remembered them.

He glanced at the photo of him, Connie and their mom taken only a year before her death and felt a pang of guilt. He didn't remember what his feelings for his family had been before the accident, but he couldn't remember ever feeling close to them, no matter how hard Connie tried to bridge the gap. Their calls just left them both feeling awkward and frustrated, and he'd rather avoid that if he could.

He fixed himself some supper then stretched out in his recliner in front of the TV, flipping through the channels until he landed on a sporting event. He didn't even care what kind most days. Tonight, it was a rerun of a golf tournament.

He reached for the journal he kept on the end table and jotted down the day's events. He'd started journaling after his accident as a way to help him recall memories. It hadn't helped. The days and years before waking up in the hospital with severe burns and no memories were still the first things he could recall. But he continued journaling anyway, using it to help him keep up with events and feelings. He'd also taken to drawing images that flashed through his memory. A particular one had been present for years—a woman with a wide smile and a little girl with pigtails. He'd dreamed of them countless times and he did his best to capture in drawing each flash of memory of them. He didn't know who they were or if they even existed. It was possible he'd met them before the accident, but it was also possible he'd made them up. Either way, these images had captured his imagination for years.

He opened his journal and flipped through to a side view of the woman he'd seen in his dreams.

He jumped to his feet, dropping the book as if it had caught fire, unable to believe his own eyes. He'd stared at that drawing too many times to count without recognition, but today, he knew who that woman was. He'd met her. He'd thought vaguely that she looked familiar, but his journal had been so far from his thoughts that he hadn't made the connection until this very minute.

The woman he'd been drawing was Isabelle Morris.

Isabelle was disappointed to discover that sleep didn't come easily for her that night. She'd been counting so strongly on finally feeling safe here, finally being able to rest. But the intruder had taken that sense of safety away. And then the sheriff's deputies had arrived, and any peace of mind she'd managed to find over the past ten years had vanished.

Oh, but how that man reminded her of Rayland.

She couldn't stop remembering his laughter. His smile. The way his eyes lit up when Kelsey hugged him. She'd dreamed about him countless times over the years. Only, tonight, when she managed to doze off, she woke less than an hour later, surprised to realize her dream had been of Deputy Drake Shaw. Her dream had changed... or had it? She pulled up a photo of Rayland on her cell phone and stared at it.

The man she'd met yesterday didn't look exactly like Rayland. A stranger looking at the two men might have seen only a superficial resemblance: same color eyes, same build, same shape to the face, and yet a number of contrasts too. His nose and jawline were different, and she'd felt scarring on his skin when she'd touched his face that Rayland hadn't had. But then there was that familiar glint in his eyes. And that lopsided way he'd smiled at her. Even the way he'd stood today. Things a stranger wouldn't notice but that a wife couldn't forget. All reminded her so much of Rayland.

She pressed her hands against her forehead. The craziness of thinking a stranger was her dead husband had her questioning herself. Rayland was gone. The stress of the threats against her must finally be getting to her. She dressed then took something for the nagging headache caused from yesterday's events.

She walked into the kitchen surprised and immediately worried to find Kelsey scrolling on her phone. They'd talked about the importance of lying low. "What are you doing?"

"Don't worry. I'm just scrolling, not posting or commenting, and I turned off the location mode." She sighed and shut off her phone, tossing it onto the countertop. "I miss my friends. School starts next week. I should be clothes shopping with Jackie and training for softball try-outs." Kelsey looked up at her. "Are we going to be back by the time school begins, Mom?"

Isabelle took her hands and held them. The truth was that she didn't know. Fleeing to the cabin had been a spur-of-the-moment decision so she hadn't really made any long-term plans. She would eventually have to return for the trial, but placing her daughter back into the crosshairs of a lot of angry people wasn't something she wanted to do. It wasn't fair for Kelsey that she might miss out on all those teenage memories, but it also wasn't fair that her daughter had become a target.

She changed the subject. "Have you eaten?"

"There's nothing to eat here."

Isabelle glanced through the cabinets and realized she was mostly right. Most of what she'd brought was non-perishables they'd had in the cupboard—and canned soup didn't make for a very appealing breakfast. They needed to stock up. "Let's get dressed and go out for breakfast. Then we'll hit the grocery store."

That perked Kelsey up and she ran back upstairs to change.

They found a local diner that served breakfast. Isabelle decided to splurge with a big stack of pancakes but Kelsey ordered only dry toast and coffee. Isabelle gave her an incredulous look after the waitress took their order and walked away.

"My daughter turning down pancakes. Are you ill?"

Her cheeks reddened and she looked away when she answered. "No. I'm just not that hungry this morning."

A text message popped up on her phone. Isabelle spotted the name Adam on it. To her horror, Kelsey picked it up, smiled, then typed out a response.

"Who are you texting? Kelsey, we're supposed to be laying low." She saw now that allowing Kelsey to keep her phone had been a mistake. If she told anyone back home where they were...

"Relax," Kelsey told her. "I know the rules."

"Then who is Adam?"

"Just a boy I met yesterday while I was walking around the lake. I came upon a group of kids hanging out and swimming. They invited me to join them. I was coming back to the cabin to ask your permission to spend the afternoon with them when I saw the police cars."

So Adam was a local. The girl had been in town all of an hour before she had met a boy. Isabelle didn't know whether to be impressed or worried. Then she remembered Kelsey's breakfast order. *Worried. Definitely worried.* "Is that why you're not eating?"

She shrugged. "Well, he's going to see me in a bathing suit, isn't he?"

The waitress brought their plates and she spotted Kelsey eyeing her stack of pancakes. Her daughter was usually very comfortable in her skin but fifteen was a difficult age.

"Well?" she asked Isabelle. "Can I go swimming with Adam and his friends later today?"

Isabelle nodded as she picked up a knife and fork and cut the pancakes in half. "On one condition." She slid the plate toward her daughter. "First, you have to help me eat this. I don't want you passing out from hunger in front of new people."

Kelsey placated her by eating a few bites while Isabelle finished what she could. She paid their bill, left a tip for the waitress then asked for directions to the nearest grocery store. It wasn't far, and they were filling up a buggy in no time.

Kelsey loaded up the cart with snacks and drinks she could offer her new friends while Isabelle focused on the staples but also snuck in some of the flavored coffee that she liked.

"Mom, look. It's that deputy from yesterday."

Isabelle glanced up to see the familiar face of Deputy Drake Shaw. Too familiar. She felt her face warm at that thought. She knew he couldn't be Rayland, yet even the way he stood now, rocking back on his heels, reminded her of him.

Kelsey hadn't seemed to notice the similarities and Isabelle wasn't surprised. She'd only been five when her father died and although she had seen many photos of him, her personal memories were fuzzy. Her eyes wouldn't catch on the similarities Isabelle was noticing—the ones that went beyond what a photograph could capture. Her mind kept telling her what she was seeing was impossible, and it was, but how could she ignore her own eyes and heart?

He was reading the label of a can of spaghetti sauce when he must have sensed them watching him. He glanced up then around until he caught her eye. He smiled and her heart stopped at the familiarity of even that small gesture.

He walked over and greeted them both. "How is it going, ladies? Any more trouble since yesterday?"

She shook her head. "No, it's been quiet. Thank you. Did you find that man you were talking about?"

"I looked but he wasn't in his usual spot. He'll show up eventually."

"Do you think he'll come back to the cabin?" Kelsey asked him, her face full of worry. She already had so much to be concerned about after the constant harassment they'd endured. Mercy was supposed to be a safe haven for them.

"I don't," he assured her. "He's used to scrounging for things from empty cabins. He probably just didn't know anyone was there. He's not a violent man—he must have just been startled."

She touched her neck where he'd tried to choke her. She wasn't buying the nonviolent part.

"I will find him and question him about the incident." He looked at Kelsey then at Isabelle. "I think he must be our guy—unless there's someone else you know of who might be targeting one or both of you."

Kelsey looked like she wanted to spill the beans so Isabelle spoke first. "There's no one," she told him. She didn't want to share the whole story with this man who was basically a stranger to them—but more than that, she really didn't think it was relevant. They'd been subjected to a campaign of harassment and threatening letters, but the Memphis police had assured her that none of the threats were credible. They had practically called her hysterical for asking if she and her daughter might be in danger. If the police back home hadn't believed she had any right to be worried, there was no reason to believe the police here would either, especially when there was no indication that Charles Jeffries or anyone involved in the case had followed them to Mercy. She didn't need to muddy the waters by mentioning it.

He seemed disappointed but nodded. "Okay, then. You have my number still if something happens. Have a great day, Kelsey, Isabelle."

Kelsey shot her a look as he walked away. "Why wouldn't you tell him, Mom?"

"I truly believe we left all that stuff behind in Memphis—and even then, no one tried to break in or attack us. How likely is it that someone would leave us alone in Memphis but then chase us all the way here? Deputy Shaw is right that it was probably this vagrant."

She glanced at her daughter's worried expression and saw that Kelsey was unconvinced.

What was the right move here? Should she try harder to reassure Kelsey that everyone was fine? Or should they maybe talk about what they'd do if they learned they really weren't safe? Would Kelsey feel better knowing that they had a plan—or would it just scare her more? She had no idea what the best option was, so for now, she just stayed silent.

She paid for the groceries, and as they walked to her

SUV, another text from Adam took Kelsey's mind off everything else. She was glad to see Kelsey perk up, but suddenly the hairs on her neck prickled. She scanned the parking lot looking for something out of the ordinary. She didn't see anything suspicious, but she felt eyes on her. She shuddered at the sudden need to get into her SUV and back to the safety of the cabin.

Someone touched her shoulder and she spun around startled.

Kelsey's eyes widened in fear. "Mom? Are you okay?"

She tried to stop her heart from racing. "I'm fine, honey." She was being ridiculous again. No one was out there. No one was following them. "What did you say?"

"Adam wants to know if I can come out. Can I, Mom? Please? It's just down the path and there will be a bunch of kids there."

She didn't like the idea of Kelsey being so far out of her sight, especially after the uneasy feeling she'd just had, but if it kept her daughter occupied and happy then she couldn't bring herself to say no. "Okay, but after the groceries are put away." They finished loading the groceries then drove home. Isabelle watched her mirrors as she drove but saw nothing worrying, which only added to her feeling that she was imagining things. There was no way anyone knew where they were. The Jeffries case hadn't followed them to Texas.

They arrived back at the cabin and Kelsey was quick as lightning unloading the groceries and putting them away, only she wasn't fast enough. A knock on the glass patio doors had them both turning. A tall, dark-haired boy wearing bathing trunks and carrying a towel draped over his neck waved.

Kelsey waved back then hurried to open the door and invite him inside. "Mom, this is Adam, the boy I told you about. Adam, this is my mom, Isabelle Morris."

He reached and shook her hand. "Nice to meet you. I appreciate you letting Kelsey come out with us."

He was polite and appreciative. She liked that. "Kelsey said there would be a group of kids?"

"Yes, about a dozen or so of us meet here every day to swim and hang out. We're just down the path toward the main pier," he said, pointing. "It's roped off for swimming."

Kelsey turned to Adam. "Just let me run upstairs and change into my swimsuit. I won't be long." She bounded up the stairs.

Isabelle watched her go then turned back to Adam. This wasn't the first boy Kelsey had shown an interest in, but she'd known all of her friends back home, and their parents, for years. "So, Adam, how long have you lived in Mercy?"

He shrugged. "Forever. I was born here. My friends and I spend most of our time by the water during the summer."

"What grade are you in?"

"Going into eleventh."

That meant he was old enough for a driver's license. Had he driven here? Or did he live close enough to walk? Would the group end up driving somewhere later, maybe to pick up some food? Kelsey was too young to be riding around in cars with a boy.

Kelsey came back downstairs and heard her last question. "Mom, stop interrogating Adam. We'll just be down the road."

"Fine, but keep your cell phone on you and don't go

anywhere else besides the swimming area. No getting into cars. If you get hungry, come back to the cabin. We have food here now."

Kelsey rolled her eyes at Isabelle's instructions but nodded in agreement.

Adam stopped at the door and turned back to Isabelle. "My parents are having a barbecue this weekend. I was hoping Kelsey could come if it's okay with you?"

Kelsey stared at her, clearly excited at the prospect. Her eyes begged Isabelle to say yes, but going to someone's house was different than just walking down to the lake to swim. On the other hand, she didn't want to disappoint her daughter. "I'll think about it," she finally told them both.

Isabelle watched her walk out with Adam. It was a beautiful sunny day. She heard the sounds of laughter and music floating on the wind through the open glass doors and smiled. She prayed Kelsey was having a good time. She deserved it.

Only, with her daughter out of the house, Isabelle had nothing to occupy her mind or distract her from the concerns she couldn't push through. She took the opportunity to grab her laptop and reviewed the briefing the district attorney's office had sent her. Her email was full of threats and angry messages from her former friends and coworkers. Their lives had been devastated by the closing of Global Health and she supposed it was easier to take out their frustration on her than on Jeffries.

She could see how she made a more tempting target for their anger. After all, Jeffries had been the local hero—the one who employed so many people, who gave to so many charities. She'd just been an ordinary employee—but she was the one who'd noticed something was wrong in their accounting. At first, she'd hoped it was just an error, and she'd reported it to her supervisor who'd gone directly to Jeffries. She'd expected them to say it was a typo or some kind of clerical error. What she hadn't expected was to overhear them talking, with Jeffries demanding that her supervisor shut her up before she became a problem by revealing everything he'd done. Her boss had come back and offered her a bribe to look the other way. She'd pretended to agree so they'd let her leave, and then she had gone straight to the authorities.

After their investigation, it had all come to light— all the fraud, all the embezzlement, the whole house of cards Jeffries had built to make the business look profitable even as he drained all its assets away. She hated that the end result had been that the company failed and so many people lost their jobs, but even if she'd remained silent, Jeffries's scheme would have been revealed sooner rather than later.

Her desire wasn't to harm the people she cared for, only to do the right thing. At first, that had meant being a whistleblower. Now, it meant testifying. That conversation she'd overheard was proof that Jeffries was fully aware of what had happened, despite his recent claims in the press that all the criminal activity had happened behind his back. Isabelle's testimony would be key in proving that to be a lie.

She reviewed the witness statement the prosecutor had sent her for errors and emailed him back the changes that needed to be made. Once that was done, she was alone with nothing to occupy her thoughts. Her mind went back to Deputy Shaw and the similarities to Rayland she couldn't ignore.

Rayland's grandfather had built this cabin and grown up in this town. She didn't know much about the man. Had he had siblings who'd also stayed in the area? Was it possible this man who reminded her so much of her husband was a distant cousin? It was the only thing that made sense.

Isabelle grabbed her keys. Her daughter would be gone for most of the afternoon so she had time to find out once and for all.

THREE

Drake was at his desk when the call from Mary McCarthy came through.

"My son was just here," she told Drake. "He says he didn't have anything to do with attacking that woman."

"I still need to question him, Mary. Can you get him to stay there until I arrive?"

"He's already gone back out to his campsite, but he said he would talk to you, Drake. He seemed coherent. Better than I've seen him in a while, actually."

"I'm on my way."

Drake grabbed his weapon then asked Josh to ride with him as backup, just in case. He loaded up the trailer to tow two ATVs to reach Benny's camp.

They passed Mary's and drove until the path ended then unloaded the ATVs. Drake headed for the oak tree where he'd been earlier. This time, he spotted Benny before they arrived. He braced himself for the encounter. On a good day, Benny seemed perfectly normal but, on his worst days, his paranoia made getting a word out of him nearly impossible. Mary had said this was a good day, but just because that had been true an hour ago didn't mean it was still true now.

Yet, this really did seem to be a good day. Benny stood as Drake and Josh approached his camp and waved to them. Drake looked him over as they neared him. He was thin and his clothes were dirty, but his camp seemed orderly and everything was in its place. "Benny, it's Deputies Shaw and Knight. Do you remember me?"

Benny nodded. "My mother said you had questions."

He seemed to understand what was going on, which was another good sign. "Yes, we do. A cabin on the lake was broken into yesterday, Benny. A woman was attacked. The man who assaulted her wore a black ski mask that I found a little ways down the hill from here. Do you know anything about that?"

He thought for a moment then shook his head. "I didn't attack anyone. I went fishing yesterday with Mike."

"Who is Mike?"

"He works for the shelter. He comes to see me once a week."

Josh leaned in to explain. "He's probably talking about Mike Spencer."

Drake nodded his understanding. He knew Spencer ran a food and clothing bank in his church. The deputies directed people to his organization from time to time.

"That's him," Benny said. "He comes to see me on Wednesdays. I was with him yesterday. I didn't attack anyone."

Drake noticed there was no mark on Benny's face either that matched the rip Isabelle had made in the ski mask with her fingernails. He glanced at Josh, who seemed to share his conclusion. "No, I don't think you did this, Benny. I appreciate your time."

They headed back to their ATVs and returned to the

SUV. Drake drove to Mary's to let her know that once they verified Benny's alibi, the matter would soon be settled.

"I don't think he was involved," he told her. "And, you're right, he seemed coherent today. He said he had a friend named Mike who came to see him every Wednesday."

Her eyes widened at that news. "I'm surprised. He won't even let me go out and see him on a regular basis. He shows up whenever he wants to."

"We think he's talking about Pastor Mike Spencer. Benny said they went fishing yesterday. We'll verify that with Spencer."

She seemed relieved at knowing someone else was reaching out to her son. "Thank you."

Once he was back at his desk, Drake called Mike Spencer, who confirmed he'd been with Benny at the time of the break-in. Drake thanked him then typed up his report with his recommendation clearing Benny of involvement in the case. While he was glad that Benny hadn't escalated to violence, that still left someone else out there who'd attacked Isabelle.

So far, they'd had no other reports of break-ins or attacks along the lake houses, and the forensic evidence had turned up nothing to help identify the assailant. He thought about how jumpy both Isabelle and Kelsey seemed and the strange glances between them. He could tell someone was hiding out when he saw them, but hiding out from what?

There was definitely something there that she wasn't telling him. Something that might have placed her and her daughter's lives at risk.

He would do whatever he needed to in order to keep them safe until he discovered who intended to hurt them and why.

* * *

The desire to find answers about Deputy Shaw and whether or not he had had any connection to Rayland gnawed at her. The courthouse would have birth and marriage records that might give her a lead. And the local library probably had a genealogy section. Or maybe there was a librarian who could help her figure out who to contact to uncover what she needed to know. She decided to try the courthouse first and see what she could learn about any siblings Rayland's grandfather might have had. A copy of his birth certificate was a good place to start.

Her phone rang as she was pulling into a parking space at the courthouse. She jumped at the sound.

For the past few weeks, she'd usually ignored the calls or sent them straight to voicemail, but this number popped up as someone she knew—her friend and former coworker Tracy Goode. They'd been close for years and she'd always supported Isabelle and Kelsey. That support was something they desperately needed now. She decided to accept the call.

"Tracy, hello."

"Isabelle, where have you been?" her friend asked, her voice high-pitched in surprise. "I went by your house and you were just gone. And you haven't been answering anyone's calls either. I was worried about you."

"I'm sorry to make you worry, Tracy, but we're fine. We just had to get away."

"Did something happen?"

"Not to me."

Her friend seemed to understand the implication. "Someone came after Kelsey? Is she hurt?"

"Just some bruising. Someone grabbed her and prevented her from leaving the locker room at the gym. They said all sorts of terrible things. They frightened her. I decided then I couldn't allow her to be dragged into this any longer, so we decided to disappear for a while." It's not like she had a job to return to.

Tracy had been one of the fortunate ones who'd found another job after Global Health folded. "That's understandable. Where are you?"

"The cabin."

She'd been on Kelsey about not revealing their whereabouts to her friends so Isabelle should probably follow her own advice. But there seemed to be no point in keeping the secret when Tracy was one of the few people in Isabelle's life who already knew about the existence of the cabin. Isabelle associated the cabin with Rayland, and bringing it up with others also meant having a discussion about a painful topic, so it was something she'd only mentioned to her closest friends.

"In Texas? You're in Texas? Wow, Isabelle, do you really think that was necessary?"

"I did what I had to do."

"Well, when are you coming back to town?"

She didn't know the answer to that.

"Kelsey has school starting next week, right?"

Tears pressed against Isabelle's eyes. She didn't want to deny her daughter the familiarity of her friends and school but she had to think about her safety as well. Plenty of kids at that school had parents who had lost their jobs—and she didn't really trust a bunch of teenagers to always be rational or fair when it came to dealing with their anger.

"Let's see how it goes."

"Well, how are things in Texas?" Tracy asked next. "Met anyone interesting?"

Isabelle's thoughts went straight to a certain deputy. Usually, Tracy was the one she would confide in, but Isabelle was still too shaken to go into details, and if she mentioned she'd met a man, Tracy would want to know everything. If she told her about the resemblance to Rayland, her friend might think she'd finally lost her grip on reality—and she might be right.

"Tracy, I have to go," she said instead of answering her friend's question. "I'll call you in a few days."

She ended the call, grabbed her phone and purse then got out and locked the car.

"Isabelle!"

She was startled to hear her name. She spun around to see Drake heading her way with a warm smile that she couldn't quite bring herself to return—not when she'd come into town with the intention of poking around in his family history. She probably should have asked him before potentially digging into his past.

She waved to him then started to cross the street to meet him. Suddenly, a car revved up behind her. She spun around to see it roaring toward her.

Isabelle screamed, fear paralyzing her as the car didn't swerve to avoid her. Someone tackled her to the ground. She hit the pavement hard, but her heart was racing so fast that she could hardly breathe.

She stared up into the piercing blue eyes of Drake Shaw and breathing became even more difficult.

"Are you okay?" he asked, concern lining his expression.

She nodded quickly but couldn't speak. He jumped up

and stared after the car that had nearly run her down. He pulled out his radio and called in the info on it while Isabelle struggled to find her composure.

Someone had just tried to run her down.

Drake ran back to her. "Do you need an ambulance?"

She found her voice. "No, I'm not hurt, Deputy."

"Call me Drake."

"Drake, I'm okay." She stared up into his face and nearly melted at how familiar the concern in his eyes seemed. She touched his cheek. "You saved me."

He placed his hand over hers and smiled. "I'm glad I was close by. I heard the car rev up then saw it was heading toward you. What were you doing here?"

Her face burned with embarrassment and she removed her hand. "I-I was heading to the courthouse." Before she could tell him about her plan, he pulled her to her feet and returned his focus to the near-accident that had just occurred.

"Did you recognize the car or the driver?"

She shook her head. "I didn't see the driver. The sun was reflecting off the windshield. But, no, I didn't recognize the car."

His jaw tensed. "Isabelle, this is the second time you've been attacked since you've been in Mercy. That's hard to accept as just an awful coincidence. Are you certain no one is after you?"

No, she wasn't sure at all. But how *could* anyone be after her here? No one knew where she was. Even Tracy had been surprised to find out she'd fled to Texas. "No one knows I'm in town, so I don't see how this could be someone targeting me."

"I wouldn't underestimate anyone's ability to track you down if they wanted."

His words heightened her fear, and she realized her hands were still shaking and her knees had started to buckle. She grabbed Drake's arm, and he held her steady before lowering her to sit on the curb.

The radio on his shoulder was crackling with information about the car but he ignored it and took the spot beside her. His manner and tone became softer, full of understanding. "I know there's something you're not telling me. Something that has both you and your daughter spooked. I've ruled Benny out as the person who attacked you in the cabin. He has an alibi for the time. And that car didn't even try to swerve to keep from hitting you. Someone is targeting you."

She stared into his face and saw he was convinced she'd been deliberately targeted, yet she still had difficulty wrapping her head around it. The police back home had assured her the threats weren't real. Now, Drake was insisting they were. "How is that possible? We left in the middle of the night. We told no one where we were going. And we've only been in town one day."

"Why don't you tell me what you're really doing here? Who are you running from? I saw the bruises on your daughter's arms. Did someone hurt her?"

So he'd seen through her evasions. Only he believed they were running for a different reason. Tears pressed against her eyes and she choked them back. "It's not what you think. We're not hiding out from an abusive boyfriend or anything like that."

"Then what is it? I've been doing this job long enough to know when two people are hiding out."

She took a deep breath and decided it was time to tell him everything. "Last year, I was working for a health care billing company named Global Health Systems. They do medical billing to private and government funded health insurance companies. I uncovered some money was missing from the accounts. I took what I'd found to my supervisor. Turns out, the CEO was embezzling money—and he wasn't doing it alone. Even my supervisor was in on it. I heard him and the CEO talk about bribing me to shut me up. I went straight to the authorities, and now a lot of the executives are under arrest. I'm supposed to testify at trial."

He nodded. "I've heard of this case. It's been all over the news. People who owned stock in the company lost millions. And it wasn't just Wall Street types who were affected—plenty of regular working folks lost a chunk of their 401(k)s."

She winced. "I hate that that happened, but I can't regret being a whistleblower. If I'd stayed quiet, Jeffries could have done even more damage. But the people back in Memphis...all they see is that the company is gone, and I'm the one who they hold responsible. In the past couple of months, I've been the target of multiple harassments and threats."

"Were any of these threats of violence? Did you report them to the police?"

"No, just vague warnings. Notes left on my car. My house was vandalized. Emails and phone calls warned me to back off. The police couldn't find any credible threats. Only, a few days ago, everything changed."

"What happened?"

"A man confronted Kelsey at her gym. He grabbed her

and told her to tell me to back off or terrible things would happen. I knew then she didn't deserve that. I had to get her away, so we packed up and came here."

"Who knew you were coming here?"

"No one. Few people even know about the cabin. I rarely talk about it, and I haven't visited it in years. I thought we'd be safe here." Now, it seemed she was wrong.

She looked at him and realized that wasn't the only thing she'd been wrong about. "I was coming to the courthouse to check up on some family history—because of you. The cabin belonged to my husband's grandfather, who grew up around here. I can't stop thinking about the similarities between you and Rayland. I was thinking maybe you're some kind of relative, a lookalike cousin or something?"

He shook his head. "I don't think that's likely. I was born and raised in Alabama. I didn't come here until four years ago. As far as I know, all of my family is from Alabama."

Disappointment spread through her. It was better, she guessed, that she hadn't wasted hours digging through records, but his answer didn't help her put to rest her curiosity about the similarities between Drake and her husband.

"I have an idea. Would you like to follow me to my house? I'll show you some older pictures of me. Maybe that will help settle it in your mind so you don't have to deal with this confusion."

The polite thing to do would be to say no, but he was offering her the opportunity to ease her mind once and for all. She couldn't refuse. "Okay, yes, I would like that."

He walked her to her car and made certain she was safe to drive before he climbed into his SUV, then he led her to a small house in the center of town. She parked on the street while he pulled into the driveway. She got out and noticed a camper taking up most of the drive.

His face reddened as he observed her noticing it. "I know it's an eyesore, but I can't make myself get rid of it. I traveled around the country in that camper and it kept me safe and sheltered for several years before I settled in Mercy."

"Oh, why were you traveling?"

He shrugged as he inserted his key into the front door lock and turned it. "I'm not sure. Just searching, I guess."

He opened the door and led her inside. His house was small but charming, neat and masculine. Books were lined up on one wall along with a row of landscape photos, most likely of his travels. She also spotted fishing equipment in the corner.

"Do you enjoy fishing?"

"It's one of my favorite things to do." He shot her a questioning look and must have realized she was comparing his hobbies with Rayland's. "Did your husband fish?"

"Absolutely. He and his dad spent hours on the lake. He had all this fishing equipment, lures and reels, and a boat that cost more than our first car." She cringed thinking of how much he'd spent on that hobby. "Actually, it wasn't just fishing. He enjoyed anything on the water."

He walked to the kitchen and poured them both a glass of water. "Well, that is something we have in common." As he handed her a glass of water, he also grabbed a photograph from the shelf.

"This was what I wanted to show you. It's me with my mother and my sister, Connie."

She glanced at the photo and felt a twang of loss. It

was definitely a picture of Drake with a different family, one she didn't recognize. He pulled a photo album off the shelf and opened it, revealing even more family photographs going back years. Other photos were visible in the house as well. Family photos of the small farm where Drake had grown up. Christmas pictures with his sister when they were children.

Pictures of Drake Shaw, not Rayland Morris.

She closed the book and shook her head. "I'm sorry. Drake, I'm so sorry."

He took the photo album and replaced it on the shelf. "It's okay, Isabelle. I can understand how surprising it must have been, seeing someone that reminds you so much of your late husband."

She shook her head. "It's not as if you look just like him, you know. You do favor Rayland but there are differences. Still, there was something about you that seemed so familiar…" She let out a sigh. "I guess I was just seeing what I wanted to see."

He motioned for her to sit and she did, sinking down into an overstuffed leather chair. He took a seat too, opposite hers. "Forgive me for asking but how did he die?"

She hesitated and he quickly backtracked.

"Never mind. It's none of my business."

"No, it's not that." She hadn't spoken about Rayland to anyone in years. It still hurt to remember how it had ended. "It was a workplace accident. An explosion at an oil refinery in New Orleans. Eight people died, including Rayland."

His eyes widened and he stood and rubbed a hand through his hair. "An explosion at an oil refinery in New Orleans?"

She nodded. "I buried a body, but it was so badly burned that he wasn't really recognizable."

"Opening the door to doubt when you come across someone who favors him," he filled in.

She nodded, feeling foolish. She'd never questioned his death before. She'd always accepted the official accident report...until she'd seen Drake. But now it was time to face the truth. Drake Shaw was not her husband. He had a life and a history that predated Rayland's death.

He turned to her, tugging at the collar of his shirt. "It wasn't Busfield Energy, was it?"

Her heart dropped at his recognition. "Yes, it was. How...?"

"I was working there when that explosion occurred. I was injured in it too—badly burned and knocked unconscious."

She gasped and pushed to her feet. "You worked with Rayland?"

His expression turned apologetic. "I... I don't know. I don't recall. Everything before the explosion is gone from my memory. But, maybe I'm familiar to you because we met before the explosion. Maybe I met you and your husband."

It was her turn to disappoint. "I never met anyone who worked at Busfield. Rayland and I weren't living together when he worked there. We'd separated."

"I need to show you something," he said. He picked up a leather-bound book from the end table then stood and moved toward her. "I don't want to confuse the situation even more but I think you should see this." He opened the book, which she could now see contained lined pages and handwritten words.

His journal. What could he possibly want to show her from his journal?

"I've been having these dreams. They're always the same. A little girl with pigtails and I'm pushing her on the swings. She's laughing with delight and there's someone else with me. A woman."

He flipped to a particular page in the journal, and Isabelle felt her pulse rush with what she was about to see.

"This is the woman I've been dreaming about. I've been drawing this same image for months now before you even came to town."

She glanced down at the drawing and tears filled her eyes. It was her. He'd been drawing her. She flipped the page and saw the drawing of the little girl with pigtails. She took out her cell phone and flipped through her photos until she came to one of Kelsey as a toddler. It was nearly an exact match to the girl he'd sketched.

She stared up at him and saw confusion in his face as he stood over her. He closed the book. "I brought you here so you could see me for who I am and put your husband's memory to rest. But I confess I can't explain how I was dreaming of you before I even met you."

He touched her arm, and she shuddered at the current between them. She stared up into his eyes. It was more than just the physical resemblance to Rayland that she'd been picking up on. She was drawn to this man like she'd been to Rayland, and she could see the same connection in his expression. He felt it too.

His cell phone rang, interrupting the moment.

He grimaced as he took it out and glanced at the screen. His face fell. "I have to take this. It's work."

He moved away from her and answered the call. She

took the opportunity while his back was to her to snap a photo of the drawing in the journal.

"On my way," she heard him say before ending the call and turning back to her. "I have to go. I'm needed at the scene of a traffic stop. The driver is a suspect in one of my cases." He took the journal from her and put it away then walked her out to her car. "I'll call you later to check in on you and Kelsey."

She climbed into her SUV, watching him as he drove away. She'd promised him that she would give up believing that he was Rayland, but that had been before he'd shown her the drawings and told her about being at the explosion. Logic told her that he couldn't possibly be Rayland, but her heart and soul had doubts.

She gripped the steering wheel as her mind spun with all this new information. It was possible that Drake Shaw was her husband.

Somehow, she made it back to the cabin. She parked and turned off the ignition to her SUV, but she didn't get out right away, still pondering all she'd just learned.

Suddenly, a scream grabbed her attention. She jumped from the car and turned in the direction of the pier where Kelsey and her friends were gathered.

She took off running, only to be met by Adam running toward her. Fear gripped her at the panicked look on his face.

"Mrs. Morris, Mrs. Morris, come quickly. It's Kelsey."

All the terrible things that might have happened to her daughter ran through her thoughts as she rushed forward. Relief flooded her when she spotted Kelsey sitting on the ground, a group of kids surrounding her. She looked pale and frightened but seemed uninjured. When she saw Isabelle, she jumped to her feet and threw her arms around her.

"What happened?" Isabelle demanded. "I heard someone scream."

Adam spoke up. "We were just hanging around listening to music. Kelsey went to get a drink from the cooler, and this man came up and grabbed her. When we heard her scream for help, my friends and I beat him off with our badminton racquets."

Kelsey sobbed into her shoulder. "I was so scared when he tried to grab me, Mama. I was so scared."

Isabelle hugged Kelsey to her, her own emotions tumbling between relief that her daughter was safe and anger that someone had tried to take her. She glanced around at the other kids and could see this incident had shaken them up too. Yet despite their fear, they'd fought back and protected Kelsey. "Thank you, Adam, and thank you all for fighting for my daughter."

"I called the sheriff's office," another of the kids told her. "We got a description of the car he was driving."

She thanked them all again then put her arm around her daughter. Adam remained close by and she didn't protest. Nothing mattered to her now except Kelsey—not the trial or the situation with Drake.

It was clear to her now that the previous incidents hadn't been coincidences, as she'd tried to convince herself. Drake was right.

They weren't safe in Mercy.

FOUR

An oil refinery explosion? That part of her story had rattled Drake. What was the likelihood that both he and Isabelle's husband had been involved in the same explosion?

His jaw tensed as he mulled over that thought.

Lord, does this mean anything?

He'd brought Isabelle over to silence any lingering question she might have about whether he could be her husband. Instead, her visit had planted seeds of doubt in his own mind. He had few memories of the days after the explosion in New Orleans and none from before that time, yet he still held the scars from that experience. He glanced in the rearview mirror at his right cheek and temple. The damage to his face and neck had healed well and was relatively unnoticeable unless someone was looking right at him, but he still had noticeable scars on the rest of his body.

But he knew who he was. He was Drake Shaw. His family history was undeniable. His sister knew who he was and his mother had known him too. How did that fit with his resemblance to Rayland Morris and his visions of Isabelle and Kelsey before he'd even met them? If he and Rayland had worked together at the refinery and known one another, it was possible he'd seen pictures of Isabelle and Kelsey, heard stories about them from Rayland, even if he'd never actually met them. But why would some old photos and stories have made such an impression on him that he'd still dream about them years later?

His radio squawked with an alert about an attempted abduction near the south side of Mercy Lake.

His gut clenched. That was close to the Morris cabin. He immediately turned his SUV and headed that way, radioing dispatch to let them know he was going to have to divert to the abduction attempt. If this incident involved Isabelle or her daughter, he wanted to be the deputy on the scene.

He spotted a deputy's cruiser in a clearing that served as parking for the public beach area before he reached the turnoff for the cabin. He pulled in behind it and hopped out. Deputy Gordon had beaten him there and was already taking down statements from a group of kids when Drake hurried over.

"Gordon, what happened here?" He scanned the area but didn't see Isabelle or Kelsey. Maybe this had nothing to do with them...but he couldn't quite convince himself that that was the case. Not when the kids all seemed to be around Kelsey's age, and it was just a short walk up the trail from their cabin.

"A man tried to grab a teenage girl. These kids stopped him and called it in."

"Where is she? What was her name?"

Instead of giving the name, he motioned to a spot beneath a tree where Drake spotted Adam with a pair of female figures. His heart dropped at the sight of them.

Isabelle was sitting on a lawn chair with her arm clutching her daughter. They both looked visibly shaken.

Isabelle stood as he approached. "What happened?" he asked her.

"Someone tried to grab Kelsey. He tried to abduct my daughter, Drake."

He reached for her arms and did his best to console her. "But he didn't succeed." He glanced at Kelsey. "Did he hurt you?"

Her eyes were wide with fright and she kept her arms wrapped tight around herself as she looked up at him. "I don't think so but I was so scared."

Adam spoke up then. "Some of us guys fought him off and pulled her away from him. He ran and got into his car. That's when we called the sheriff's office."

"Good thinking. I'm glad you were all there with her."

"I gave a description to Deputy Gordon, as did some of the others."

"Did you recognize him? Was he wearing a mask?"

"No mask, but he was wearing a ball cap, so I didn't get a good look at his face. But he didn't look familiar and he had out of town plates."

"Did you notice from where?"

"No, I didn't. I just knew it didn't look like Texas plates."

Which made it less likely that this attack was a fluke or the work of a local criminal. He glanced at Isabelle and wondered about the court case she'd told him about. Was her boss the type of person to send someone across state lines to terrorize her into not testifying? It was an angle they would need to explore more thoroughly after this.

But, first, he needed to get them to safety. "How about

Adam and I walk you both back to the cabin. Deputy Gordon is taking statements from the others. I'll let him know to meet us there."

Isabelle nodded then stood and helped her daughter to her feet. She didn't release Kelsey from her grasp as they headed to the cabin, with Adam following along behind them. Drake conferred quickly with Gordon, who then returned to taking statements. He was going to have a time speaking to all those kids then notifying their parents about what had occurred. Drake should offer to help, but making certain Isabelle and Kelsey were safe was his top priority.

Drake kept a close eye out for anything out of the ordinary as they walked to the cabin. Isabelle's car was parked out front but the door was standing open, sending his guard up. He motioned to it. "Did you leave the car like that?"

She stopped to look at it then shrugged. "Maybe. When I heard someone scream, I just came running."

Drake motioned for them to stay back, then walked over and took a quick glance inside before deciding nothing was amiss. Her purse and cell phone were still in the car and the key was on the ground. Satisfied it was like she said—she'd been so frantic at the thought of Kelsey in danger that she'd hurried off without locking up—he picked up the keys and shut the door. Still, he wasn't taking any chances. He had them wait a few moments more while he cleared the cabin.

He breathed easier once the cabin was secure, and he let them inside then pulled out his notebook and asked Kelsey to tell him in detail what had happened, jotting down notes as she explained.

"I was hanging out with Adam and his friends. We were having fun. Listening to music, swimming, laughing. I got thirsty, so I went to get a drink from the cooler in the back of Jake's truck. That's when the man grabbed me. I screamed and tried to hold on to the truck as he yanked me away but he was too strong. He picked me up and carried me toward his car but I kept fighting him. Then I saw Adam and several of his friends running toward us. They tried to tackle him but the guy didn't let go. Finally, someone was able to pull his arm away from me long enough that I slipped out of his grasp. Adam grabbed me and we ran back toward the beach." She glanced up at Adam who continued the story.

"The guy took off for his car with my friends chasing him. He hopped in and took off. That's when I found my phone and called 911."

Drake was proud of Adam and those boys. They'd likely saved her life. "Had you noticed this man hanging around earlier? Any idea how long his car had been in the parking area?"

Adam and Kelsey glanced at one another then both shook their heads. "We didn't notice," Adam continued. "But, to be honest, none of us were really paying any attention. We were just enjoying our group time. There were at least a couple dozen vehicles in the lot. We wouldn't have noticed another one."

Small-town folks usually noticed out of towners, but during the summer months plenty of tourists visited the lake so they probably wouldn't have given a stranger a second look. Besides, these kids had been too caught up in their own good time to pay attention to anything out of the ordinary happening around them. It wasn't a criticism, just fact. They had no way of knowing how long this predator had sat there and watched for his opportunity to grab Kelsey.

"Did you recognize him?"

They each shook their heads no.

"Can either of you describe him?"

"He was a big guy," Adam said, prompting Kelsey to echo his phrase.

"Yes, a big guy."

"He was a head taller than me, but between his ball cap and sunglasses, I couldn't see much of his face." Adam sighed then gave an apologetic shrug. "I wasn't really looking at him. Mostly, I just remember the terror in Kelsey's eyes."

His words prompted Isabelle to stand and walk a few steps away. Her hand over her mouth and the tremble of her shoulders told him it was taking all she had to hold it together.

He closed his notebook. They'd given him all they could. Hopefully, Gordon had uncovered more.

When he arrived at the cabin door, Drake excused himself and stepped outside to speak to his fellow deputy. "Did you get anything?"

The statements he showed Drake parroted much of what Kelsey and Adam had said but, again, no one could give a solid description of the assailant.

"I've already called in a BOLO on the vehicle based on the kids' descriptions," Gordon stated. "Looks like the plates were from out of state but no one could agree on which one. The plates were blue with white lettering, so I'll have to do some research on that."

He thought about the case against Isabelle. If this assault was related to her case then it was probably someone from her life. "Try Tennessee," he suggested. "That's where Isabelle and Kelsey are from."

Gordon agreed that was a good place to start. "Several of the kids had their phones on them and videoed what happened. I'm having those images emailed to Jana. No one caught the complete tag but hopefully Jana can piece it together."

Jana Carter was in charge of their IT department and an expert at breaking down video footage. "Good. If she finds something, we can add it to the BOLO. If she finds an image of the assailant, have her send it to me. I'll see if Isabelle recognizes him."

He suspected these attacks had more to do with her past than anything she'd encountered in Mercy. He needed to update Sheriff Thompson. These attacks had taken place in their county and it was up to their department to keep Isabelle and Kelsey safe.

He thanked Gordon then phoned the sheriff to update her. She agreed they needed to figure out who was behind the attacks against Isabelle and Kelsey.

He walked back into the cabin and faced Isabelle. "You've already told me few people knew about the cabin." He looked at Kelsey and got her attention. "And did you tell any of your friends you were in Mercy?"

Her eyes widened but she shook her head. "I wanted to tell my best friend, Jackie, but I didn't. She begged me to tell her but I promise I didn't tell anyone."

After the near abduction today, he doubted she would lie about that. "Well, there are a lot of ways someone could have found you here. I'll check your car for a tracking device. I also want to take your cell phones. Our computer expert can look them over, make sure no one was tracking them and that they're safe to use. It shouldn't take but a day or so. I'd feel better knowing she gave the okay."

Kelsey looked horrified. "You want me to give up my phone?" She jumped to her feet and turned her stare to her mother. "Mom."

Isabelle too hesitated at his suggestion. "I thought about taking it from her when we left but it didn't seem fair for her not to be able to contact her friends at all. Besides, Drake, we need a phone. What if something happens and we need to call for help? There's no longer a landline in the cabin. I had it disconnected years ago."

"Kelsey can use my phone," Adam offered. "My mom will let me borrow hers for a day or two, at least until you get yours back," he told her.

Kelsey still seemed to struggle with parting from her device, but she reluctantly took it from her pocket and handed it over.

Drake was glad for Adam's offer. "And I'll leave you with a burner phone to use. At least, we'll know you're not being tracked," he told Isabelle.

"But he already knows we're here," she replied. "He's already tried to grab Kelsey. He must know we're staying here."

"Maybe. But if he is tracking your phones, it's still a good idea to make sure he can't use them to track you when you're away from the house—maybe in a location where you'd be easier to attack." He met her eyes, and he knew they were both thinking about how she'd nearly been run over.

"Is it even safe for us to stay here?"

Kelsey looked stricken at her mom's words, and Drake

could tell she didn't want to go. He didn't like the idea either. If the two of them left, how would he be able to make sure they were safe? The same guy tracking them could find them again—and Drake wouldn't be there to protect them.

"There are no guarantees—but I can promise you that we're on your side here. That's not something you can necessarily count on if you go somewhere else. Make sure the doors are locked, the alarm is set, stay inside, and call me immediately if anything happens. Just to be safe, I'll ask the sheriff to increase patrols near here and watch for anything suspicious."

That seemed to be enough. She reached out and touched his chest in a gesture that seemed instinctive. "Thank you, Drake."

"My pleasure." He covered her hand with his as his heartbeat increased at her touch. If she'd fallen into his arms as she looked like she wanted to, he would have gladly pulled her into an embrace.

It was time to go.

He bagged both their cell phones and planned to take them right to Jana. Hopefully, she could give them the once-over quickly and get them returned to them.

He headed to his SUV, being sure to scope out the area as much as possible. The kids had dispersed after the incident and Gordon had contacted all of their parents.

Drake climbed into his SUV and headed down the road to the closest convenience store, where he picked up a burner phone for Isabelle to use, then returned to the cabin.

"I'll get your phones back to you as soon as possible.

In the meantime, call me immediately if you need me or dispatch."

"Thank you for everything, Drake. I mean it. You don't have to be this nice to me."

She touched his arm again, and he covered her hand with his, sparks sending his head reeling. A big part of his job was helping people and he was always glad to do so, but his desire to be there for her went greater than duty and he couldn't explain why. He wasn't her husband, yet he also couldn't explain how drawn to her he was or why he'd dreamed about her face all these years. Nothing made sense to him, except for his bone-deep drive to make certain nothing happened to her.

He broke away from her then turned to Adam. "Do you need a ride home?"

"No, I have my mom's car," Adam said.

He took the time to phone Adam's parents and update them on what had happened, assuring them that he was fine and on his way home, then headed toward the sheriff's office as the kid walked to his car parked in the public lot.

Jana was still in her office going through videos Gordon had collected from the kids when Drake arrived. "Finding anything?" he asked her.

"Not much," she admitted. "I have a lot of videos, and several of the kids captured images of the man who tried to grab Kelsey, but none of them are complete. I'm trying to build a composite of him based upon all the different angles."

"No one got a clear view?"

"No. There was a lot of chaos, and he apparently appeared out of nowhere. He must have been watching them for a while before he struck, and he picked his moment well."

"Thankfully, he didn't succeed."

She nodded then pulled up the composite she had so far. "Meet our attempted kidnapper. Once I'm done, I'll run him through facial recognition and see if I can find an identification."

"What about the license plate of the car?"

"I was able to piece together the plate numbers but it came back as a stolen plate."

That news didn't surprise him. "Don't forget to distribute it to the patrol units too and add it to the BOLO. Someone must know him or have seen him around town. And send me a copy. Isabelle or Kelsey might recognize him."

She nodded. "Gordon mentioned that. I'll do it."

He pulled out the cell phones he'd confiscated from Isabelle and Kelsey. "I was hoping when you got the chance you could look through these phones and see if there's any evidence this guy used their phones to track them here."

She picked up Kelsey's and looked it over. "Do they have GPS?"

"Yes, but they claim it was turned off."

"I'll double-check and get them back to you in the morning."

"That soon?"

"I'm going to be here for a while working on this composite. We need to find this guy before he skips town."

"Thanks, Jana."

"No problem."

He walked back to his desk and fell into his chair. Something Jana had said struck him about the abductor skipping town. He didn't think the attacker was going anywhere. He'd made a play for Kelsey and it hadn't been successful. If someone was really trying to kidnap her or threaten Isabelle into not testifying, they wouldn't give up so easily. This perpetrator might leave town with the job undone, but Drake knew in his gut even if this guy left, another bad guy would show up to try again.

They needed to find out who was behind these attacks before one of them was successful.

Isabelle awoke to a noise. She jerked awake and sat up in bed. It was dark outside but she glanced at the clock and saw it wasn't that late. Barely midnight.

She grabbed the burner phone and saw she had a missed call from Drake. She quickly phoned him, hoping nothing was wrong.

"I'm sorry to wake you," he said. "Jana called me. She says your friend Tracy has been calling your phone over and over again. I was worried it might be something important."

She breathed a sigh of relief. Tracy was notorious for calling until she got an answer, and since she didn't know the police had Isabelle's phone, she was probably panicking at not being able to reach her. "Thanks for letting me know. She's probably just worried about me not responding. I'll phone her and let her know we're safe."

"That's good. Do you need me to send you the number?"

"No. Tracy has been my emergency contact for years. I have her number memorized."

"Okay, then. I'm on duty tonight and patrolling close by so call or text me if you need anything."

She smiled at his overprotectiveness then pressed the

red button to end the call. Her face warmed at how much she'd wanted to press her face into his shoulder earlier and let him comfort her.

Her mind was still reeling from all that had happened, but Drake's appearance in her life was the most unsettling. She closed her eyes and tried to picture Rayland but saw Drake instead. Was it because she was misremembering or was Drake Shaw really that much like her husband?

She wasn't imagining the similarities. And given that he'd admitted to being hurt in an explosion—the same one Rayland had died in—it was possible his injuries had changed his appearance too. The photos she'd seen of him with his mother and sister prior to the accident didn't look quite the same as the man he was now. Yet, he had a strong family history of being a Shaw, complete with childhood photos of him and his sister and family who knew him.

It was just an odd coincidence.

A cruel joke, God.

What could be less funny than thrusting her into danger then sending a man who reminded her so much of her dead husband to her rescue?

She got up and walked to the window and stared out at the lake. It was truly lovely from this view. The brightness of the moon cast a glow on the water. Everything about this cabin should have been peaceful and safe but that wasn't how it had turned out. She thought again about leaving…but where would she go? She couldn't run away from her problems forever. And if she went somewhere else, Drake wouldn't be there. As frightening as the attacks had been, he made her feel safe. Confused, but safe.

She spent a minute wishing she had someone she could talk to about this—but then she remembered that she did.

Tracy had been a good friend. Maybe confiding in her was just what Isabelle needed.

She picked up the phone then dialed her number. Her friend's tone was questioning when she answered, but when Isabelle identified herself, Tracy was relieved to hear from her.

"I was worried about you and Kelsey. I've been calling your phone for hours and you haven't answered. Why are you calling from this number? What happened to your phone?"

"We're in trouble, Tracy. Someone followed us here from Memphis. He tried to abduct Kelsey so the deputy confiscated our cell phones to try to see if they were being used to track us. This is a burner phone for me to use in the meantime."

"What do you mean someone tried to abduct Kelsey? Is she okay?"

"She's fine. She was with some friends when this man tried to grab her. They fended him off."

"Who would want to hurt Kelsey?"

"You know who. Charles Jeffries. I think he's sent someone to harm us to try to stop me from testifying."

"Are you sure it's Jeffries? They indicted several members of his management team. For all we know, he had no idea what was happening. At least, that's what I've heard he's claiming."

Isabelle had never told Tracy about overhearing Jeffries admitting his involvement or the bribe he'd tried to offer her. "I know differently, Tracy, and that's what I'll be testifying to. Without me, a jury might believe him. He might walk free."

Tracy was quiet for a moment as she took in this new information. "Then you shouldn't do it."

She was stunned by her friend's reply. "What?"

"You can't risk Kelsey's life for someone like Charles Jeffries, can you? Just tell the prosecutor you can't take the risk."

"I can't do that. His actions have hurt a lot of people. He needs to be held accountable for them."

"I know you have this obsession for doing the right thing, Isabelle, but this is your daughter. What will you do if they harm her?"

She hadn't expected her friend to focus in on the major doubts Isabelle was already struggling with. Now she really didn't know what to do.

"Honey, I know you want to set a good example, but this is dangerous. Jeffries is a dangerous man. He could send people after you."

"I think he already has." She didn't mention the other attacks against them. She was more certain than ever that the break-in and the attack in the street were not unrelated events.

She'd tried so hard to be a morally upstanding person. After the way she'd allowed things to deteriorate with Rayland, she'd fought so hard not to make another mistake and to teach her daughter that honesty and respect were more important than anything else.

"Tracy, there's something else. This deputy who's been protecting us—"

Tracy squealed with delight. "You met someone? That's wonderful news, Isabelle. What's he like?"

Exactly like my dead husband.

Or, at least, the best version of himself. By the time

she'd asked Rayland to leave their home, they'd both taken a deep detour from the people they'd meant to be. He'd become so irresponsible, and she'd become prone to nagging her husband whenever he didn't do things her way. She now knew that had just been her way of trying to control every situation. As a single mom, she'd finally had to face the truth that not every situation was under her control. She regretted now that she hadn't been more patient with him, hadn't tried harder to really listen to what he was saying instead of turning everything into a fight.

Their marriage had faced serious difficulties after his parents' deaths. In his grief, he'd avoided making decisions and consoled himself with expensive toys and adventures—cars, motorcycles and even a boat that they really couldn't afford. While he was having fun, Isabelle had been trying to salvage their financial future. She had been left to step in and handle the estate they'd inherited, including selling the family's construction business. Despite having worked there for years, Rayland had wanted to leave it all behind rather than taking over running it, the way Isabelle had expected. But she hadn't argued against his decision. She'd just stepped up and shouldered the load of handling the sale, and she'd been good at it too. Suddenly, the real differences in their personalities had surfaced, which had created a wedge between them. Their relationship had suffered and neither had tried hard enough to repair it. It had taken a separation and the risk of losing his family for Rayland to get serious about restoring their relationship. Taking the job at Busfield at the recommendation of a friend had been his way of proving to her that he could be responsible. Even though it meant them living separately, Isabelle had been in favor of the idea. At the time, she'd thought of it as the first step in separating their lives. It was only once he was gone for good, killed in the explosion, that she'd realized how weakly she'd fought to save her marriage. She'd turned to God and cried out for a second chance. Joel 2:25 had been her Bible verse, her lifeline. She'd clung to the promise that God would return to his children what the locusts had eaten, all while knowing that, for her, the real second chance she longed for would never come.

There was nothing she could do about how her marriage to Rayland had gone. She could only move forward alone. That was a lesson she'd had to learn a long time ago.

Tracy knew she'd been widowed but she didn't know about Drake. She opened her mouth to explain but before she could utter a word, a noise from outside grabbed her attention.

It sounded like a splash.

She pulled back the curtain and looked out at the lake again. Water was moving and she spotted something floating. It was too dark to tell for sure, but it looked like a pink jacket…just like the one her daughter always wore.

"Hang on," she told Tracy. Fear rushed through her that her daughter might be in danger, but she tried not to rush to conclusions. Surely Kelsey was safe inside in her bed.

Isabelle flung open her bedroom door and rushed across the hall to the bedroom Kelsey was using. She pushed open the door, stunned to find the bed empty and her daughter's jacket missing. "No!" she cried as the fear she'd been holding back slammed into her.

"What's going on?" Tracy asked as her breathing intensified.

"I have to go," Isabelle cried, hanging up and rushing

down the steps, every inch of her praying her daughter was in the kitchen or vegging out in front of the television.

Kelsey was nowhere to be seen, the security system had been turned off, and the back sliding door stood cracked open.

She'd gone outside.

Anger rolled through her. Her daughter's impulsiveness had overridden her common sense. What on earth would cause her daughter to risk going outside unprotected?

Isabelle slid open the door and stood on the porch. "Kelsey!" Her voice was loud even to her own ears in the silence of the night. "Kelsey, where are you?"

No response.

She ran down to the water and heard a splash again. She opened her cell phone and used the flashlight feature to move over the water. It was definitely a pink jacket floating in the water with an overturned canoe nearby.

Panic gripped her and she ran into the water, swimming out to the floating object. She looked around frantically, but saw no other evidence that her daughter was in the water.

Suddenly, someone grabbed her leg and yanked hard.

Isabelle gasped for air as she went under.

FIVE

Isabelle flailed around, trying to push herself to the surface. She heard muffled screams from above and her mind went to Kelsey. Her daughter was in trouble. So was she.

She saw a light in the murky water then a figure below. It was a man and he was intentionally pulling her under.

He reached for her arm to hold her down, away from the surface. He was too strong for her to fight against but that didn't stop her from trying. She kicked and flailed at the figure. Her lungs felt like they might explode at any moment, but the man did his best to keep her from surfacing. With her kicks and punches failing to affect him, she did the only thing she could. His hand was on her shoulder, so she craned her neck and bit him, hard. He released his grip on her and she managed to push to the surface, gasping for air the moment she broke through the water.

"Help me," she cried as the strong hands pulled her under once more.

There was more splashing in the water, and moments later the man released her. She surfaced again and struggled to catch her breath and tread water, coughing and gasping. Another pair of strong hands grabbed her and she flinched.

"It's okay. I've got you." The voice was husky and weighted with worry, but she knew it instantly.

Drake.

She stopped fighting and went limp in his grasp as he towed her back toward the bank of the lake. When he could stand, he swooped her up into his arms and carried her. She did the very thing she'd wanted to do earlier, dug her head into his chest and clung to him, thankful for his quick action and strong embrace.

At that moment, it didn't matter whether or not he was Rayland. All that mattered was that he was there for her.

"Mama!" Kelsey's voice cut through her disorientation, and she turned her head to find her as Drake placed her gently on the grass.

Kelsey flung herself into her arms and Isabelle hugged her. "Where were you?" she asked as the initial surge of relief turned to concern. "You weren't in your room. I was out looking for you."

Kelsey's face reddened and she turned her head. Isabelle followed her gaze and spotted Adam standing nearby. "We weren't doing anything but talking. We were on the walking path when we heard you cry out."

"I thought you were in the water. I saw your jacket floating and the boat overturned."

Kelsey gulped hard. "I'm fine, Mama. I'm sorry I worried you." Guilt and worry clouded her expression as she came to realize the depth of the mistake she'd made. Kelsey often acted without thinking of the consequences. It was a trait she shared with her dad.

She pulled Kelsey into another hug, grateful that she wasn't hurt even though Isabelle really wasn't okay with her sneaking out. They were going to have a long discussion about that. That wasn't okay even when their lives weren't in danger.

She turned to look at Drake. Water dripped from his dark hair but he pushed it back. She spotted his boots a few feet away and realized he was barefoot. He'd jumped in to rescue her, and the memory of being carried in his arms was both familiar and new and exciting.

"Drake, what are you even doing here?"

"I was patrolling nearby and heard Kelsey's screams for help."

He would have had to have been very close by to hear that but she was thankful that he had been. "It was a man. He was trying to pull me under to drown me."

He nodded as he wiped water from his face with his palm. "I know. I saw him." He stood and hurried to his boots. Beside them were his radio and phone. "I'll call it in. We'll need to search these woods. He didn't have an air tank so he would have had to come out of the water somewhere close." He made the call for assistance then scanned the area himself. "You and Kelsey should get inside in case he comes back."

Kelsey helped her to her feet and turned toward the house, but Isabelle walked over to Drake. Something bothered her about the whole situation and she could see the same doubts on his face. "How did he know to be in the water? He obviously pulled the boat out and overturned it and used Kelsey's jacket to lure me in, but how could he know I'd even see it? What if I hadn't spotted it before morning? Surely he couldn't have stayed out there all night. How did he even know he'd have a chance to sneak into the house to get her jacket in the first place?"

"I have my jacket," Kelsey interrupted.

Isabelle turned and realized her daughter was wearing the very pink jacket she thought she'd seen in the water. It hadn't been hers in the lake but one similar.

"That answers one question. But how would he even know when I would look out the window?"

He scanned the area before turning back to her, his jaw clenched. "Because he's got eyes on you somehow. He's watching."

The thought terrified her. She hurried Kelsey and Adam into the cabin and locked the doors, peeking through the curtain as Drake, gun drawn, vanished into the woods. Red lights flared outside the front windows as several sheriff's office vehicles arrived. The other deputies spread out and joined in the search.

She heard them moving around outside. After she dried off and changed, Isabelle did her best to stop her hands from shaking. She'd nearly died tonight and it was only because of Drake that she hadn't.

Whoever Charles Jeffries had sent after her had nearly completed his mission tonight. That had been too close.

Drake's dreams were always the same. Isabelle laughing, her face full of joy while pushing a little girl on the swing. The squeals of laughter from the child floated up to meet him and an overwhelming feeling of happiness radiated through him as he approached the pair.

"You have to know sneaking out wasn't okay," a voice said, pushing through his dream and pulling him awake. He opened his eyes and realized he was in the cabin on the couch. He'd stayed over last night after he and other deputies had searched for the man who'd attacked Isabelle in the water. It had ended without any success, and Drake felt the need to stay and make sure there wasn't another attack. He was just glad Gordon had had a dry uniform in his car that Drake had been able to borrow. He'd also been able to provide Isabelle with a new burner phone since hers had been lost in the water when the assailant had pulled her under.

He sat up and glanced around. Isabelle and Kelsey were in the kitchen but he could see them through the open door. Isabelle was at the stove cooking while Kelsey sat at the bar. The girl rolled her eyes as her mother chastised her for her actions the night before.

"I didn't go very far," she insisted. "We were only talking."

That wasn't good enough for Isabelle. "It doesn't matter what you were doing. You put yourself at risk by sneaking out of the house and you nearly frightened me half to death. You've got to think about the consequences of your actions."

"I will."

"It had better not happen again."

"It won't," Kelsey responded.

This simple exchange between mother and daughter told Drake a lot about their relationship. Isabelle's parenting style struck him as strict but warm, and while Kelsey seemed annoyed by the discipline, she was not physically or emotionally harmed by it. It was obvious they were close.

Isabelle spotted him watching and smiled, a beautiful smile that lit up her face. Her long blond hair was pulled up into a ponytail that only accentuated her swan-like neck. "I hope we didn't wake you."

He forced himself to stop staring. "No, not at all." But

the memory of his dream and the sound of her laughter had him wanting to hear it in real life. He stood and stretched then walked into the kitchen. "Everything okay this morning?"

Kelsey shrugged, but it was Isabelle who spoke. "Yes, everything is fine. We both slept better knowing you were around." She poured him a cup of coffee and handed it to him. "I scrambled some eggs. Can I offer you some?"

"No, thank you. I want to get to the sheriff's office and check in with Sheriff Thompson. We need to figure out a plan to keep you both safe."

"You're leaving?" Both pairs of green eyes looked at him with concern.

"Just for a little while. I asked Deputy Gordon to come by and stand guard while I'm gone. He's a good man. He'll make sure you're safe."

He saw Isabelle's uncertainty about him leaving, and it made him feel good to know that she preferred having him around. He was leery too of giving over the reins of their protection detail to someone else but it had to be done. They needed a plan to combat these threats against Isabelle and Kelsey, and if he wanted to be included in the decision making, he needed to be the one to meet with the sheriff. Besides, he trusted Gordon and all his friends in the sheriff's office. They'd become his family over the past several years since he'd settled here in Mercy.

He glanced at Kelsey, who'd hardly eaten a bite of the food in front of her, then leaned across the counter toward her. "How about you? Are you holding up?"

She shrugged as if his concern was unnecessary. "I'm okay."

"Are you sure? You've been through a lot in the past few days. It's all right to be frightened."

She looked up at him, her eyes hard with anger. "I said I'm fine."

"Kelsey!" Isabelle's voice was stern. "Don't be rude. Drake is only trying to help us."

The teenager pushed to her feet as all the emotion she'd probably been bottling up finally burst out. "I don't want his help. I want this to be over. I want a normal life again." She marched through the door and up the stairs.

Isabelle's face flushed. "I'm so sorry about that. I'll make her apologize."

"Don't worry," he assured her. "I can handle a few angry words." He better than most understood what it was like to have your life spiral out of your control. During his recovery, he'd been forced to rely on his sister to even do basic things for him. It was a situation he hadn't enjoyed and regaining his independence had been a necessity. "I don't blame her. I know what it feels like to have your world turned upside down."

Isabelle tried to put on a brave face, but he could see from the set of her jaw that she was barely hanging on. "Her emotions are all over the place lately and she doesn't think before she acts. She's not coping well. I was glad when she met Adam, but now he's just one more reason for her to get distracted and not think about the consequences of her actions." She turned to place the pan and utensils she'd used to cook into the sink, but he suspected her real reason for turning was to gather her emotions where he couldn't see.

He recalled how she'd felt in his arms last night as he'd carried her from the water. Once he'd gotten past the panic and rush of adrenaline, the weight of her cradled against his chest had felt so natural. The memory of his dream returned to him and the images of her smiling. He wanted to see her do that in real life. That full of life, eyes lit up, teeth-showing smile. And he wanted to hear her laugh. Aside from keeping her safe, he wanted to make that his goal.

He started to reach out to her but thought better of it. "She's a teenager. It's a difficult age even when your life isn't in peril. I'm sure she's not intentionally being defiant."

"No, she's not. Her heart's always in the right place. But she can be impulsive, and having good intentions won't make a difference if something happens to her, will it?" When she glanced back at him, fear and worry still clouded her expression even as she did her best to mask them.

He wondered briefly if seeing him and being reminded of her husband added to that pain. He turned away from her and walked into the den to gather his things, chastising himself for even having those kinds of thoughts about her. She was beautiful and strong and amazing, but looking at him and being around him must also be a source of grief for her. He needed to get this case settled, figure out who was targeting her and why, then end the threats so she could get on with her life without him around as a constant reminder of what she'd lost.

He heard a car in the driveway and immediately tensed and placed his hand on his gun at his hip. He walked to the window and glanced out, relieved to see Gordon's SUV pull into the driveway and park.

It was time for Drake to go.

He saw Isabelle standing in the kitchen doorway. "It's Deputy Gordon. I'll brief him then be back as soon as I can," he assured her.

She turned to him and flashed him one of those pressed-lipped smiles that didn't reach the rest of her face. "We'll be here."

It felt wrong to leave her but also wrong to remain with her.

He walked out and spoke to Gordon, who assured him he would keep watch until Drake returned.

Drake drove to the sheriff's office to find that Sheriff Thompson was in her office with the door closed. Josh stopped him before he knocked. "She's on a call. She'll be out to discuss the situation once she's done."

Drake glanced down at his rumpled shirt. "Maybe I'll go clean up while I wait. Holler at me if she's ready before I finish."

Josh agreed, and Drake hurried to the locker room. He had a fresh uniform in his locker and managed to wash up, shave and change before the sheriff was ready.

"Don't you look better," Josh teased him.

Drake grinned and tossed a piece of paper at him.

"Any more problems last night?" Josh asked.

"No, it was quiet. Whoever grabbed her is still out there, and I'm worried that he's watching her somehow. It doesn't make sense that he knew she would be watching the water at that hour."

"Well, we've canvassed everyone near the area and no one saw anything out of the ordinary. It was late though, and the cover of darkness aided him. Only..." Josh paused and sat up in his chair as he leaned toward Drake. "I don't have to tell you that this incident doesn't really fit with our burglar theory."

Drake had figured that out too. "No, that was pretty obvious when he tried to abduct Kelsey. He's targeting her. He set a trap for Isabelle and she walked right into it."

Josh nodded. "Sheriff Thompson is on the phone with the prosecutor in charge of the case Isabelle is testifying in. She's trying to get all the details about who might be after her."

Drake grimaced. "We *know* who's after her, don't we? Her boss. He must be the one behind this."

Sheriff Thompson's door opened and she walked out in time to hear Drake's statement. "Don't be so certain," she told Drake. "I just got off the phone with District Attorney Kennedy. She says there have been eyes on Charles Jeffries for the past two weeks. He hasn't left town."

"So he's not the one who followed her to Mercy, but so what? From what I've seen of him on the news, he would hire someone to do his dirty work," Drake pointed out.

"Yes, Kennedy agrees that he's definitely that type," Sheriff Thompson stated.

"What I don't get is why he'd go this far," Drake continued. "They must have other evidence against him without Isabelle putting her life in danger."

"They do, but she's the only one who's willing to testify with direct evidence that Jeffries was involved. He's trying to shift the blame to one of his managers and claim it all happened behind his back. Without her testimony, the case against Jeffries is at risk."

"Her life is at risk," Drake reiterated.

Sheriff Thompson saw him getting agitated and held up her hands. "I know that. And it's still our job to keep her safe. I'm going to assign Josh to finish looking into any possible local threats. Once we've ruled them out, we'll know that she brought this danger with her to Mercy."

Josh leaned forward. "Well, we've already confirmed Benny's alibi for the break-in, and he doesn't match the description of the man who tried to abduct Kelsey, so we can rule him out as a suspect. Jana came up with a composite image of the man who attacked Kelsey." He picked up a piece of paper and handed it over. "We've distributed this to all patrol units and deputies and Jana is trying to identify him using facial recognition."

Drake glanced at the composite. Unfortunately, not much of the man's face was visible. The ball cap and sunglasses had shielded him very well. Still, at least it was something. "I'll show this to Isabelle and Kelsey to see if either of them recognizes him. Maybe we can ID him as one of Jeffries's men. If that's the case, it'll be easy to tie him to this."

"Good," Sheriff Thompson stated. "Keep following those leads, Josh. In the meantime, Drake, I want you to stay with Isabelle and her daughter and keep them safe. Around-the-clock protection for them. No one's going to get them while they're in our jurisdiction."

He was glad she agreed with him on that point, but he couldn't continue sleeping on the couch. The cabin probably had a third bedroom they weren't using, but remaining downstairs meant he could better hear if someone approached. He had another thought. "I have a small travel camper. I can pull it up to the cabin and stay in it. That'll give them some privacy while I can still be around all the time—and keep an eye on the exits."

The sheriff gave that idea consideration before giving

the okay. "That's a good idea. Josh and I will keep checking in with you regularly and I'll assign Deputy Gordon for backup. If you see anything or need more help, let us know." She turned and walked back into her office.

He dropped in to see Jana, who welcomed him with a smile despite the bags under her eyes from working overnight. "Hey, Drake."

"Hey, Jana, I was wondering if you were able to examine Isabelle and Kelsey's cell phones?"

She nodded and reached for a plastic bag containing both phones. "I did. I couldn't find any evidence that either phone was being tracked, but I did clone them both in case something else comes up. For now, I've made certain the GPS is blocked. No one is going to be tracking them using these."

He thanked her then hurried outside to his SUV and climbed inside. Before he started the engine, he took out his cell phone and called the new burner phone he'd given Isabelle.

"Hello?"

He found that he smiled automatically when she answered. "It's Drake. I'm almost done at the sheriff's office."

"So you're coming back to the cabin?"

"Yes, but first I need to go by my house. Sheriff Thompson has ordered around-the-clock protection for you and Kelsey, so I had the idea of bringing my travel camper and setting it up in your driveway."

"So you'll be close by?"

"I will. Is that all right with you?"

She hesitated a moment, but it didn't strike him as an awkward silence. Instead, he imagined the small lift of her lips as she welcomed his involvement. "I'm glad it's you, Drake," she said finally.

"Me too." Though he still wondered if she was really okay with that. The question about him being her husband still felt unresolved. He was sure he knew who he was... and yet he still couldn't get past the fact that he had been dreaming about these two before he'd even met them. He didn't know what that meant and it bothered him. Did it bother her too?

"I'll be there as soon as I can." He ended the call then drove to his house and backed into his driveway so he could hook up the travel camper. He'd made this purchase before leaving Alabama using part of his settlement from Busfield. He'd lived in it while traveling around the country looking for someplace to call home. Arriving in Mercy, it hadn't taken him long to realize this was where he wanted to be. It had instantly felt like home, and after going through the law enforcement academy and joining the sheriff's office, he'd used the remainder of his settlement money to purchase his house. The camper hadn't moved from the driveway since and he'd even thought about selling it.

Now, he was glad he hadn't. It was once again going to come in handy.

It didn't take him long to get the camper hooked up and ready to go. Then he went inside and packed a bag with clothes and necessities. He didn't know how long he would have to be away, but he wanted to be prepared. The trial was in just over a week, so if Charles Jeffries was trying to keep Isabelle from testifying, he had a limited amount of time to make it happen.

He glanced at a photo on his shelf of him and Connie

and realized he'd never called her back. It would have to wait.

He drove to the cabin. Once there, Isabelle and Kelsey came outside and, along with Gordon, helped him set up the barriers and lights and trail cameras around the property then hook up the camper. The ladies gave the inside a quick tour then exited with approval.

"It's cozy," Isabelle stated. "Plus, I love the finishes."

He beamed at her approval. "I bought it used then updated the floors, cabinets and countertops myself to make it feel more like home as I traveled."

"You did the work yourself?" Isabelle asked. "Do you like doing construction and working with your hands?"

He saw a slight hesitation in her. Was this another point where she'd compare him to Rayland? Was carpentry something else they had in common? "I do," he admitted. He imagined she was adding it to some kind of mental tally, but for his part, he didn't think it proved anything. Lots of people enjoyed working with their hands.

Gordon helped Drake secure everything then said goodbye to Isabelle and Kelsey. "I'll stay close to the phone in case you need me," he told Drake before climbing into his cruiser and driving away.

Kelsey pulled out her phone then glanced up at Isabelle. "Mom, Adam is texting. Can he come over?" The girl's face held so much excitement that he knew she wouldn't say no. It seemed to give Kelsey a sense of assurance to know she had a friend willing to stand by her.

"Sure," Isabelle agreed, and Drake noted Kelsey was still glowing when Adam's car pulled into the driveway minutes later. He must have been waiting at the public parking lot for her okay.

She bounded toward him as he got out of the car, and Drake saw real concern in Adam's expression.

"I'm better now," Kelsey assured him.

"You have a right to be shaken up," he said. "That was a close call. Do you know why someone is targeting you and your mom?"

She shook her head. "We think it has something to do with my mom's job. She's testifying against her boss and he might have sent someone to try to stop her."

Adam's eyes widened and he glanced at Isabelle with admiration before turning back to Kelsey. "That's heavy stuff. I'm glad nothing bad happened to you. I was hoping we could still hang out together. If your mom is all right with it, of course." After sneaking out with Kelsey the previous night, he had to know being upfront was the only way he was going to be allowed around anymore.

Kelsey turned and looked at her mother, who looked conflicted. Drake knew she didn't want to let the girl out of her sight again but was probably trying to figure out a way to voice it without sounding neurotic or somehow blaming Adam for what had happened. "I don't think it's a good idea for Kelsey to leave the safety of the cabin."

Drake had a counter suggestion that might appease everyone. "Once I settle in, how about I grill us up some burgers and we can all watch a movie inside?"

Kelsey turned to look at Adam, who seemed okay with that suggestion. "That sounds like fun," Adam said.

The boy probably knew it was the best he was going to get. Isabelle's mama bear instincts had kicked in, and it was unlikely that she was going to let the girl out of her sight again for quite some time.

"Can I give you a hand, Deputy Shaw?"

Drake shook his head. "I'm almost done here. Why don't you two go on inside. Isabelle and I can finish up."

Kelsey turned to her mother, who nodded her agreement. The kids hurried into the cabin. Isabelle turned to Drake. "Thank you for suggesting that. I know Kelsey likes that Adam kid but I just don't think it's a good idea for her to go off somewhere with him."

"I agree. We have to be careful. But Adam is a good kid and it doesn't hurt to have another set of eyes on Kelsey." And he'd already observed that Adam could hardly take his eyes off the girl. Drake couldn't blame him. He was having his own difficult time prying his eyes off her mother.

He unpacked his belongings then made a perimeter sweep before heading back inside the cabin, where the two teens were stretched out on the couch. Kelsey had the TV remote in her hand and they were scanning through movie titles, looking for something to watch and commenting on each suggestion. They finally settled on a superhero flick to watch, then Adam helped Drake light the grill for burgers while Isabelle and Kelsey readied the patties.

It was a humid summer afternoon, but the breeze from the lake helped keep the temperature bearable. Drake placed the burgers onto the grill then walked back inside. Kelsey and Adam had claimed most of the space on the main couch so Isabelle patted her hand on a spot beside her on the love seat. He slid into place, momentarily worried that he might be so captivated by the scent of her shampoo that he would let the food burn. She didn't help the matter either when she leaned against him.

As he'd expected, the scent of her hair rattled through him, causing his every thought to be of her. The long shape of her neck. The fullness of her lips. He laid his arm over the back of the couch, and even the way she seemed to fit into the crook of his arm seemed natural and right.

Only, he noticed she didn't seem to be having the same reaction to him as he was from being so close to her. Isabelle rarely took her eyes off Kelsey even as they watched the movie. She couldn't seem to relax for a moment, and he couldn't really say he blamed her. He didn't have a child but if he did and someone had tried to hurt her, he was certain he wouldn't let his guard down either. Someone had already broken into this cabin once, but he was determined he wasn't going to let that happen again. They were safe here and they would remain so.

"I'll go see if the burgers are done," she said, standing and walking out onto the deck. He watched her open the lid to the grill. Grease popped up from the meat and she jerked her hand away and cried out in pain.

Drake sprang to his feet and was at her side in a flash. He touched her hand to examine it. It was a small burn, painful but nothing to worry about, but the feel of her hand in his and the way she looked up at him with her tear-filled eyes awoke something inside of him.

Isabelle fingered the small burn on her palm. It was nothing compared to the real danger they were facing but Drake hadn't treated it like it was nothing. He'd comforted her, and she still recalled the feel of his hand in hers as he applied the burn cream.

She felt her face warm. She was reminiscing about him applying burn cream to her hand. What was the matter with her?

She hadn't given another man a second glance in all

the years since Rayland had died, but Drake was different and it wasn't just the resemblance. She felt drawn to his kindness and compassion for their situation. Some had criticized her for turning on her boss but Drake showed nothing but admiration for her courage. She liked that. She also liked that he seemed to be there whenever she needed him.

Unlike Rayland.

She winced at that negative thought. She'd done her best to focus on only the best qualities of her late husband when thinking of him and especially when speaking about him to Kelsey, but he had been far from perfect. He'd had an impulsive streak that often clashed with her desire for order and organization. He'd spend money without thinking and would bring home toys and games without even considering the cost. As young parents, their finances had been tight. As tragic as the loss of Rayland's parents had been, she'd thought maybe some good would come of it if the inheritance meant that they'd have some financial security, but she and Rayland hadn't agreed on what to do with the money. She'd wanted to save it but Ray had preferred to spend it—often on frivolous, unnecessary purchases. It had been the cause of many arguments between them and, ultimately, her push to ask him to leave.

She still remembered the way he'd kissed and hugged Kelsey before picking up his duffel bag, walking to his car and driving away. He'd phoned her several times over the next few months, telling her about his job working at the oil refinery in New Orleans. Each time, he'd asked her for a second chance, but she'd never given him an answer. Even though she still loved him, she'd convinced herself that their problems went too deep to be fixed. She'd given up on their marriage, which was something she regretted the moment she learned about the explosion and that he was never coming home again.

She'd spent a lot of time nursing her regrets and praying for God to give her a second chance to prove she knew what really mattered. Irritations that had seemed so important to her then now seemed silly and irrelevant, and it saddened her to remember how she'd focused so much on those things instead of fighting to save her marriage. She'd clung to God during those dark days and to His promise in Joel 2:25 that He would return to His people all that the locusts had eaten.

She might one day get that second chance at marriage, and this time, she would fight to protect those she loved.

It was dark outside when Adam and Kelsey parted ways and he drove off. Drake also said good-night to Isabelle and Kelsey. He waited until they'd gone back inside the cabin and locked the doors before he walked the perimeter of the property. Since Isabelle owned the land, the sheriff's department had been able to erect barriers. He made certain they hadn't been moved and no one was sneaking around out there before he walked to the camper and went inside.

He pulled out his laptop and typed up notes about the security measures they'd taken then submitted the report for Sheriff Thompson to review tomorrow morning. He checked the trail cameras and saw nothing out of the ordinary. Everything seemed secure for the night. He leaned back on the small camper-sized sofa and closed his eyes. He couldn't relax but he also couldn't remain awake twenty-four seven. He had everything secured and he was a light sleeper. He would know if someone crossed onto the property.

He awoke to an alarm and immediately reached for his gun, though he reminded himself not to rush in without checking out the situation. In these woods were plenty of wildlife that roamed at night and could have set off the alarms. At first, that was what he thought he'd heard. He glanced at the trail cams and his heart jumped as he spotted movement near the front entrance. Someone was on-site.

He called for backup then hurried out of the camper, gun raised as he scanned the area. He heard movement behind Isabelle's SUV and headed that way. A hulking figure lay on the ground next to her vehicle.

"Don't move," Drake shouted, but it did no good. The man jumped to his feet and ran. Drake chased after him for several moments but the assailant was fast. He quickly vanished into the woods. Drake contemplated his next action for only half a second. Protecting Isabelle and Kelsey was more important than chasing after this guy. Besides, backup was already on the way. Perhaps they would catch him as he was running to his car.

Car.

He'd been on the ground beside Isabelle's SUV. What had he been doing? Cutting the brakes? Somehow tampering with her fuel lines to make her more vulnerable to attack? Or something much worse?

He grimaced as he darted back toward the SUV. He heard the door to the cabin open and saw the porch light come on before Isabelle and Kelsey stepped outside. Their crumpled clothing and bleary eyes told him they'd been awakened by the ruckus. Kelsey remained by the door but Isabelle walked down to meet him.

Drake held out his hand to stop her. "Don't," he warned. "Get back."

He had a bad feeling in the pit of his gut. He knelt and looked beneath the vehicle where he'd found the intruder. His heart sank at the sight of wires and C-4 attached to a cell phone. A bomb—one that the intruder could detonate at any time just by placing a call.

Drake jumped to his feet and screamed at Isabelle and Kelsey. "Get back! Get inside! It's a bomb!"

Isabelle turned and ran toward the cabin, calling for Kelsey to run inside. The girl did as commanded and made it inside. Isabelle was nearly to the porch, Drake only a few feet behind her, when the bomb exploded.

SIX

The ground shook beneath Isabelle's feet as the bomb exploded. Debris rained down all around her. She dropped to the ground and covered her head. Her ears were ringing from the sound of the blast but she vaguely heard someone calling her name. She glanced up and saw Drake jumping to his feet and running toward her. He reached her and rolled her over, checking to make certain she hadn't been hit by flying debris.

"I'm not hurt," she said, but the words were muffled even to her own ears.

He lifted her to her feet and pushed her toward the cabin. The heat from the fire was intense and she glanced back to see. Her car was on fire, as was his camper, and the flames soared up into the night sky. Once inside, he slammed the door then stumbled across the floor. He wasn't walking steadily so she hurried and put his arm across her shoulder so she could help steady him as they made their way to the couch. Once he was sitting, she realized he was hurt. Blood was flowing from a gash on his head.

"Kelsey, get some towels," she cried, and her daughter, still wide-eyed with shock from the explosion, ran into the kitchen and returned with a roll of paper towels. She tore off several pieces and handed them to Isabelle, who pressed them to the wound.

He grimaced at the pressure. "I'm okay," he assured her, his hand covering hers to take over control. "Are you sure you're not hurt?"

"No, I'm fine." She turned to her daughter, who was still standing behind her, staring in shock. "Kelsey, go and get my cell phone. We need to call the sheriff's office for help and an ambulance for Drake."

Kelsey turned and ran up the stairs, returning a moment later with the cell phone. Isabelle handed it over to Drake and he dialed the sheriff's office.

"Allison, this is Drake. I need fire and rescue personnel. A bomb attached to Isabelle's vehicle exploded. It and my camper are on fire. We're all fine inside the cabin." He listened then ended the call. "Help is on the way."

She examined his head wound. "You probably need stitches." She removed the paper towel that was now red with blood and examined the gash.

"I'm fine," he insisted. "Head wounds always bleed a lot. I'm sure it's not as bad as it looks."

She tore off another piece of paper towel and tried to apply it to his wound, but he seemed agitated and kept pushing her hand away. "I said I'm fine," he insisted.

"Drake, stop fussing and let me treat you." He was getting unnecessarily irritable and restless, something Rayland used to do too when life spun out of control.

"I said I'm fine, Izzy," he barked. "Leave it alone."

His words rocked her and she stepped back, too stunned to even reply for several moments. She could only stare at him, scarcely able to believe he'd used that name. "Why did you say that?" she demanded.

He looked up at her shaky tone, now confused. "I'm sorry I raised my voice but I'm—"

"You called me Izzy."

Confusion still lingered in his eyes as he tried to recall. "I did? I'm sorry. It just came out."

He didn't get it. He really didn't understand. "No one calls me that... No one but Rayland ever called me Izzy."

He stared at her mouth agape for several moments before understanding dawned on him. He shook his head. "I'm not him, Isabelle. We've already determined that."

"Did we?" Yes, she remembered the pictures he'd shown her of his life as Drake, but hearing that nickname flow so instinctively from his mouth was making her head spin with confusion.

Before he could offer further comments, sirens and lights approaching the cabin interrupted the moment. "I should go meet them." He pushed to his feet and darted out of the cabin without another word about the matter.

Isabelle cleaned up but her hands were still shaking at the shock of hearing that name again after all these years. Her father had sometimes called her Bella, which irritated her mom who'd always insisted that Isabelle was so much more sophisticated. She hadn't been allowed to have a nickname—until that had changed with Rayland. He'd labeled her Dizzy Izzy right from the first time they'd kissed because he'd said her kiss made his head spin. It had eventually just been shortened to Izzy over the years. Now, to have Drake use that nickname at a time when he was injured and upset—a time when he seemed to be running on pure instinct—had her once again pondering what it all meant. She didn't know yet, and she didn't really have time at the moment to dwell on it, but it seemed yet another indicator that this man, this Drake Shaw, might be more than he believed himself to be.

Kelsey was at the window watching the scene unfold. Isabelle walked over and peeked out too. The fire was still roaring, and police and ambulance lights filled the sky along with the glow of the flames.

"Can we go onto the porch and watch?" Kelsey asked.

She agreed but then opened the door to find the smoke overpowering. She closed it back again. "We're too close. We should stay inside," Isabelle said instead.

A breeze could send embers toward the cabin, which might cause it to catch fire, so they couldn't relax as they watched the local first responders battle the flames. Her SUV was a total loss, burned right along with Drake's camper.

The assailant had upped his game and tried to kill her again. She was glad Drake had seen and stopped him or else the next time she used her vehicle, it might have been for the last time. That feeling of dread sat in the pit of her stomach, eating away at her sense of peace, but it was now entangled with another feeling that caused her even more confusion and stress.

Because, no matter how hard she tried, she couldn't explain away Drake's use of Rayland's nickname for her.

Izzy.

Why had he called her that?

He marched toward the sheriff's vehicle, asking himself that question over and over. He hadn't even realized he was saying it until she'd freaked out over it. It had seemed such a natural thing to flow from his lips at the time. How was he to know that no one but Rayland ever used that name?

I'm going to call you Dizzy Izzy because your kiss makes my head spin.

A vague memory of him saying that came to mind. But when would he have said that to her? And why, given that he hadn't even kissed her yet? But he knew he didn't need to kiss her for his head to spin. Just being near her had the same effect on him.

"Drake, how are you?" Deputy Max Hampton asked him as he approached the vehicle.

"I'm a little rattled but I'm okay." He still had the paper towel pressed against his head. He was sure it was blood soaked by now but he was equally sure it was nothing a few stitches couldn't fix. "Where's the sheriff?"

"On the way along with half the county's emergency response team."

He gave his report to Hampton as the first official deputy on the scene then walked to the ambulance himself to have his wound looked at. Meanwhile, he instructed other deputies to scour the area for the man Drake had seen planting the bomb.

The paramedic cleaned and proceeded to stitch up the gash on his head. It hurt and his ears were still slightly ringing from the explosion, but he was more concerned with what this recent attack meant for Isabelle and Kelsey's safety.

They couldn't remain at the cabin.

It was time to move them somewhere the sheriff's office could control. Somewhere no one would be able to find them.

When Josh and Sheriff Thompson arrived on the scene, they found Drake still sitting with the paramedic.

"How are you?" Sheriff Thompson asked.

"I'm okay," he assured her. "We're all fine."

"My partner is inside the cabin checking out the woman," the paramedic explained. "But it looks like your deputy took the brunt of the force."

He grimaced. He'd made it sound like he'd shielded Isabelle with his body to save her. He wished he'd gotten that far. He shuddered at what might have happened to her.

"I saw the guy placing it on her vehicle. It had a cell phone trigger. Likely homemade. He probably intended to wait until she was in the car to set it off but he must have realized he was caught so he set it off right then. Isabelle had come out of the cabin when she heard me chasing the guy I suppose."

"We have patrols out searching for him based on the description you gave but, so far, there's no sign. I'm sure he used the explosion and fire as cover to slip into a car he had parked nearby."

Drake nodded. That was what he'd figured too. "I didn't go after him because I didn't want to leave Isabelle and Kelsey unprotected."

Sheriff Thompson touched his arm. "You did the right thing, Drake. You kept them safe."

"Not for long. It's obvious we can't defend the cabin, Sheriff. We need to move them to someplace safe."

"Josh and I were talking about the same thing. We'll bring them to the sheriff's office while we locate a safe house."

"Good."

"I'll go inside and break the news to them," the sheriff

continued. "They'll need to pack a bag. Once you're able, Josh, pull my SUV around to the side."

She walked away and Drake watched her enter the cabin.

Isabelle wasn't going to like having to leave, but he knew she would do whatever it took to keep her daughter safe.

"I'm sorry about your camper," Josh stated, and Drake glanced at the now smoldering mess that used to be his home.

"It doesn't matter," he said truthfully. Until the previous day, he hadn't used it once since coming to Mercy. It was a product of his past and Mercy was his present and his future.

He stared at the cabin and was suddenly struck with gratitude that Isabelle and Kelsey were safe. He couldn't explain how important they'd become to him in such a short time. And he also couldn't wrap his brain around how and why he'd pulled the name Izzy from his mind.

It was possible his past wasn't as settled as he'd once believed.

Isabelle wasn't surprised when Sheriff Thompson entered the cabin and asked to have a word with her, but she was concerned that Drake hadn't come too.

"He's fine," the sheriff assured her. "He's being stitched up by a paramedic."

A different paramedic had checked her over and left minutes before. Her only lasting effect was a slight ringing in her ears that had already started to fade.

"Can I get you something, Sheriff? Coffee or tea?"

"No. There's no time. We need to move you and your

daughter to a safer location right away. I'm going to need you both to go and pack a bag. We need to leave as soon as possible."

"Is something wrong? Is the cabin in danger of catching fire?"

"No, the fire department has sprayed down the cabin and they've mostly battled the fire, but whoever placed that bomb might be out there. We want to take you back to the sheriff's office until we find a safe house, and I'd like to do it while it's still dark so prying eyes can't follow us. We'll also need to confiscate your cell phones for the time. You shouldn't have any outside contact with anyone besides me and my deputies."

That made sense to Isabelle and seemed to be the right thing to do. This explosion only proved that the man that was after her could get to her here. The cabin was no longer safe.

She turned to Kelsey. "Go and pack a bag."

Only Kelsey wasn't as convinced. Despite the danger, she only saw what she was leaving behind. "What about Adam? I won't get to see him or even talk to him."

Isabelle felt bad about that. Kelsey had already been forced to give up her life and friends in Memphis. Adam had been the one person who'd made this entire ordeal easier for Kelsey, but their safety had to take priority over Kelsey's new friendship.

Sheriff Thompson interjected. "I'm sure we can arrange something," she told Kelsey. She looked at Isabelle and smiled. "Adam's a good kid. He'll understand."

Isabelle hoped that was true, because she could already see that Kelsey didn't understand. "Mama?" Her tone was demanding and it rubbed Isabelle wrong. She had no time for childish arguments. Enough was enough. They had to focus on practical matters like safety.

"I said go pack a bag," she told her again, this time with her own commanding tone. If her daughter was going to act like a child, Isabelle would treat her as one.

Kelsey bunched her fists in frustration but marched upstairs without another word.

"We'll be down as soon as we can," Isabelle told the sheriff before hurrying up to her own bedroom and stuffing some clothes and toiletries into a duffel bag. She hadn't brought much with her from Memphis but she was leaving most of that behind.

"Ready?" the sheriff asked as Kelsey appeared in the doorway.

She nodded, and the sheriff turned to Isabelle, who also agreed. "We're ready."

She used her radio to alert her deputies that they were on the move.

They followed Sheriff Thompson to her SUV. Kelsey climbed into the back seat while Isabelle took the front seat and the sheriff slid behind the wheel.

As she drove past, Isabelle saw the devastation at the front of her house. Her SUV was a smoky, blacked-out mess, and Drake's camper was only a shell. The fire department was still spraying both with water, and black smoke raised to the sky. The house was also surrounded by ambulances, fire trucks and sheriff's office vehicles.

Tears formed in her eyes at the devastation. Someone was trying really hard to keep her from testifying and this was an homage to their determination.

It was too much.

They arrived safely at the sheriff's office and Sheriff

Thompson led them to the break room. "It's not much but there's a TV and decent sofa. You should be comfortable while we make arrangements for someplace to put you."

"We'll be okay," Isabelle told her.

Kelsey fell onto the sofa. Isabelle could see that she was near tears, but it wasn't clear if it was because of what had happened at the cabin or because she was being separated from her phone and her new friend.

Isabelle sat beside her and put her arm around her. Kelsey leaned into her and cried softly. "Everything is going to be okay," she told her daughter even though she wasn't truly sure of that herself. She knew Jeffries was behind these attacks, but the looking over her shoulder was getting tiring. She didn't want Jeffries to get away with his misdeeds, but she also didn't want to have to keep fearing for her or Kelsey's safety either.

Kelsey soon cried herself to sleep and Isabelle let her stretch out on the couch. She walked to the vending machines and found herself a cola and a pack of M&M's to munch on. She wasn't hungry but it at least gave her something to do with her hands while they waited.

It wasn't fair to put Kelsey through any of this. She hadn't done anything wrong—she shouldn't have to suffer because Charles Jeffries believed he should be allowed to get away with defrauding people. Maybe it would be easier to just call up the district attorney and tell them she was no longer willing to go to court.

She didn't want to do that. In fact, it felt so wrong to allow Jeffries to get away with terrorizing them, but she had to think about their safety.

She was still mulling over the idea when Sheriff Thompson appeared at the doorway. She walked in and pulled up a chair at the table where Isabelle sat. She glanced at Kelsey and purposefully kept her voice low so as not to wake her. "She seems to be sleeping fine. How about you? How are you holding up?"

Isabelle shrugged. "I'm relying on the M&M's to get through."

Sheriff Thompson smiled then held out her hand, and Isabelle tapped a few into her palm. "It's difficult worrying about them, isn't it?" she asked motioning toward Kelsey.

"Yes, it is. I want to keep her safe, but doing what's best for her might mean letting a bad man go free."

"Are you thinking of not testifying?"

"After all this, wouldn't you? I can't allow my daughter to be harmed."

"I understand that."

"Do you? Do you have children, Sheriff?"

She nodded then took out her cell phone and pulled up a photo. It showed a small child with black hair and big blue eyes. "He's four and a handful but he's the most important thing in my life. There's nothing I wouldn't do for him."

"Then you do know."

She nodded. "I can't tell you what to do, Isabelle, but I can promise you that we will do whatever it takes to keep you and your daughter safe. Besides, how do you even know refusing to testify will stop this? It may be too late for that."

She popped another handful of M&M's into her mouth and chomped on them as she considered. She couldn't make this decision tonight but she didn't want to make the wrong choice.

Sheriff Thompson's phone buzzed with a message. She

glanced at the screen. "Looks like they've got a plan together. I need to go approve it." She reached across the table and took Isabelle's hand. "We will keep you both safe. I promise."

She appreciated Sheriff Thompson and took comfort in her words. She seemed to really care, and that said a lot about a leader.

A half hour or so later, Drake appeared. He'd cleaned up but was still sporting a bandage on his forehead. Isabelle was still nursing her candy and soda at the same table. He slid into the chair across from her, then reached out and held her hands.

"How are you holding up?"

She wanted to reassure him, but she also wanted to be honest. Her chin quivered with all the pent-up emotion she was trying so hard to control. "I'm scared," she admitted.

He didn't let go but squeezed her hands tighter. "I know you are, but I've been thinking about it and I don't believe your coming here was an accident. God brought you here so we could protect you."

She'd wondered about God's plan in all of this. Had God brought them here for her safety or so she could find Drake and be reunited with her husband? He was still denying he was Rayland, yet her heart was telling her differently. His eyes were Ray's. They shared the same hobbies, the same one-sided smile. Plus there was the matter of him using that nickname for her. She had no explanation for the how or why he had been identified as someone else, but she was ever more convinced that Drake Shaw was actually her husband, Rayland Morris.

"We've arranged for you and Kelsey to stay at a motel on the outskirts of the county. It's isolated and we were able to snag two rooms. We deputies will take shifts in the second room, but we want to keep your location limited to who knows even among the sheriff's office."

She was glad that it sounded like he was going to remain close by. She liked the sheriff and the other deputies she'd interacted with, but she trusted Drake. "Okay, if you think that's what's best. We're ready."

"I do."

She stood and walked over to the couch and shook her daughter awake. "It's time to go," she told her. Kelsey roused and rubbed her eyes before standing and gathering her belongings.

They exited through the back entrance then climbed into yet another vehicle. Drake drove this time and Isabelle watched as the landscape went by. She hadn't had time to really look at the area but it was beautiful, especially in the early morning hours. Even the lake the cabin sat on was picturesque. It was a shame they were too busy running for their lives to be able to enjoy it.

Now she wished she'd taken advantage of the beauty and the luxury of the lakeside cabin for her and Kelsey to enjoy over the years rather than just using it as rental income. She'd been so busy trying to survive raising a child alone that she hadn't taken time to really enjoy what she'd had.

Drake pulled into a small motel off the highway. The single-storied place held lines of rooms that formed a box with a courtyard in the middle and a pool off to the side. There were no businesses around and she'd seen no houses either. This place truly was isolated and obviously catered to highway traffic, since the off-ramp was nearby.

He put the SUV into Park in front of the office. "Wait here. I'll run inside and get the keys."

They waited as he marched into the small office then returned a few minutes later with two plastic key cards. He pulled the SUV to a parking spot and they got out. Isabelle and Kelsey carried their bags while he used the key card to open a door at the end of a row. Isabelle and Kelsey followed him inside. As he cleared the room, Kelsey dropped her bag on one of the two double beds. Drake made sure the room was secure, then opened the door to the adjoining room and glanced around before tossing his own bag onto the bed.

He turned back and Isabelle nodded. "This will be fine," she told him.

She walked over to Kelsey and placed her arm around her daughter, pulling her to her and hugging her. "We'll be fine here. We're safe."

He must have sensed how difficult this was for them because he shifted from foot to foot before offering to give them some space.

"Josh—that is, Deputy Knight—is coming by later to bring us some food. If there's anything specific you'd like to eat, just let me know. I'm going to go call the sheriff and let her know we made it safely."

He closed the adjoining door, leaving her and Kelsey alone.

Kelsey leaned her head into Isabelle's shoulder and sobbed.

Isabelle allowed herself to shed some tears as well for the predicament they'd found themselves in.

Their lives were in danger and they were stuck in a motel, but at least they were together.

* * *

The next two days dragged on for Isabelle. The deputies brought lots of greasy fast food, snacks, books and magazines to help occupy their days. Isabelle couldn't concentrate long enough to read and the TV seemed to be airing nothing but nonstop boring shows.

Drake brought his chessboard and challenged Kelsey to a game. That perked her up for an hour or so but then she was back to moping. He reluctantly returned her cell phone so she could listen to her downloaded music only after he'd removed the sim card. Without Wi-Fi, which they didn't have at the motel, she couldn't use it to contact anyone. She still squealed with delight when he handed it to her, hugged Drake then put in her earbuds and tuned the adults out completely.

"At least she'll be content for a little while," Isabelle said. She joined him at the table with the chessboard. "I'm not very good. Rayland was teaching me before..." She'd been going to say before she'd asked him to leave. Playing chess had been one of the last fun things they'd shared before their marriage started falling apart. "Before he died."

They took turns making moves without speaking for several turns before Isabelle sighed and leaned back in her chair. Even she was starting to get bored. "What do people in Mercy do for fun?"

He grinned then shrugged. "We have plenty of things to do. Unfortunately, most of them require you to be around people and out in the open, which in your case isn't a great idea."

"I wasn't thinking about now—although I would do nearly anything to get out of this room for a few hours. I was actually just trying to imagine what a regular weekend would look like."

"There's the movie theater, the bowling alley, anything lake related. There's also a great café downtown that makes an amazing steak. In the spring and fall, there are festivals that are fun, and every summer the Mercy County Sheriff's Office and the next county's sheriff's office have a charity baseball game to raise money for school supplies for underprivileged kids."

"That sounds like fun."

"It is. You already missed it this summer. It was weeks ago."

"Did your team win?"

His face reddened. "Unfortunately, the London Sheriff's Office beat us this year. We were missing one of our star players, Deputy Mike Tyner."

"What happened to him?"

"He met a woman from the FBI, fell in love and followed her back to Houston. I was happy for him at the time but that was before I realized we were missing a great shortstop. Unfortunately, I was a poor substitute."

She smiled at the image he painted of Mercy. "It sounds like a nice place to live. At least when someone isn't trying to kill you."

"I like it. After my mom died, I spent a lot of time traveling around looking for someplace where I felt like I belonged. I found that when I came to Mercy. These people took me in and welcomed me as one of their own."

Tears sprang to her eyes and she quickly blinked them away. "That sounds nice," she admitted. Nothing at all like her home in Memphis, where her job had pitted her against her coworkers and everyone had been out for themselves.

Kelsey had found a decent group of friends, but the gossip among her friend group, and especially her friends' moms, had run rampant. Isabelle had done her best to stay above it as best she could, but the more she thought about returning to that life, the less she wanted to.

"Are you thinking about moving here?"

He winked at her as a way of letting her know he was teasing, but she realized that, maybe, she *was* thinking about it. What did she have to go back for? A bunch of people who treated her like a pariah?

Drake's expression grew serious. "As much as I'd love for you to stay...do you really believe you could be happy here looking at my face and knowing I'm not him?"

"Are you completely sure you're *not* him?" She studied the chessboard then moved a piece. They hadn't really talked about him calling her Izzy but she hadn't forgotten it. She'd been watching him too for the past few days, watching his stance and his mannerisms for something familiar. Everything about him was familiar.

He rubbed a hand over his face. "I thought we'd settled that."

"We haven't even spoken about the most recent revelation, Drake. You called me Izzy. Rayland always called me that, and I can't help but think how easily it came to you when you were under duress, like it was an instinct or a memory."

"There's no memory, Isabelle. There's nothing there. When I try to remember my life before the explosion, it's an empty hole of nothingness. But I also can't deny that my sister and my own mother knew me—as Drake. Yes, maybe I favor your husband and maybe we were both at that refinery the night of the explosion, and, yes, maybe

I'm drawn to you in a way I can't explain…" He stopped and choked back a knot of emotion in his throat. "But how do I get past my own mother recognizing me?"

She saw he was struggling with this as much as her and wished she could provide some definitive answer. Instead, she reached across the table and held his hand. "I don't know, but how do you get past your wife recognizing you?"

His eyes searched hers but his cell phone buzzed before he had to address her question.

He pulled his hand from hers and checked his messages. "The prosecutor on your case wants to meet with you to do witness prep." He stood. "I should go call Josh and work out a plan to make sure the location is secure."

He walked into the adjoining room and closed the connecting door.

He probably thought he'd gotten out of continuing that conversation, but as far as Isabelle was concerned, they weren't finished with it. She wasn't going to let this go until she knew how it had happened.

Isabelle did her best not to disturb Kelsey, who had fallen asleep listening to music, but the girl roused. "What's happening?"

"We need to go into town to meet with the prosecutor to prep me for my testimony."

She pulled her earbuds from her ears. "And I have to go?"

Isabelle was surprised at her question. She'd thought Kelsey would jump at the opportunity to get out of the cramped, confining room. "I'd rather have you with me."

She didn't argue the matter but got up and readied herself.

Drake knocked on the adjoining door. "Everyone decent?"

"Yes, come on in," Isabelle said.

He'd been on the phone with Josh for the past hour making arrangements, and she could see he was more tense than he had been earlier. "They wanted to bring you back to Memphis but Sheriff Thompson convinced them you were safer here in Mercy, so they agreed to make the trip. We arranged to meet them at the courthouse."

"When?"

"They'll be in by this afternoon. Josh and Gordon are prepping the area where we'll meet with them, upping security procedures at the courthouse just in case. Thankfully, the sheriff's department oversees courthouse security."

She was thankful for all the precautions his team was taking.

"What about when it's time for me to testify? The case is going to court in less than a week. I'll have no choice but to return to Memphis then."

He reached out and touched her hand. "We'll figure that out when the time comes. Don't worry. I won't leave you alone. I'll make certain you're taken care of even if it means I have to make the trip myself."

She was beginning to believe that the only way she would feel safe again was with Drake by her side. He had no jurisdiction to make arrests in Tennessee, but he could still be there to protect her—and you didn't need to have jurisdiction to stop someone from attacking. She could insist on him coming as a condition of her testimony.

She was looking forward to getting this entire ordeal behind her, but she knew the closer the trial date came, the more pressure Jeffries would place on her to prevent her testimony. She'd thought a lot about the sheriff's words and had accepted that backing down wouldn't be enough to keep her safe. Jeffries would always be afraid of her telling her story to anyone and being believed. The only way she'd be safe was if her word was in the public record—and he was held accountable for what he'd done.

Besides, even though threatening her daughter might have frightened her, letting an evil man like Jeffries go free when she could stop him was unthinkable. Choosing to testify against him was the right thing to do.

She would just have to trust in Drake and his team to keep her and Kelsey safe.

He didn't like taking Isabelle out into the open but it couldn't be helped. The prosecutors needed to go over her testimony and they'd insisted on a face-to-face meeting. The only alternative had been to bring the prosecutor to the motel, and Drake hadn't been keen to that idea either. He didn't know these people or what leaks might occur in their office, so he was glad when Sheriff Thompson had arranged this meeting on their terms and turf.

He shuffled Kelsey and Isabelle into the car then headed back toward town. Kelsey was still tuning them out with her earbuds, which he'd figured out was one of her coping methods. He didn't take it personally. Isabelle was quiet too, so he reached over and held her hand.

"Are you ready for this?" he asked her.

She shrugged. "It doesn't matter. I have to do it. Besides, this is the only way I'm going to get my life back, isn't it?"

It was true. So far, they hadn't been able to identify

or locate the man they believed had been targeting her, which meant each day she was at risk. Once the trial was underway and her testimony was done, there would no longer be any value in silencing her.

They just had to make it to that point.

Gordon had gone ahead to help secure the location. Drake had alerted Josh that they were on their way. He'd declined any backup. No one knew about the motel except for Josh and Gordon, and Drake preferred to keep it that way. He did, however, radio Josh to update him on the route they were taking.

He'd thought it was safe until he turned onto a back road. He glanced in the rearview mirror and tensed as a truck he'd noticed behind them earlier also made the turn. He sped up and the other vehicle did as well, never coming close enough to be on their bumper but also not allowing the distance between them to widen too far.

They were being followed.

Isabelle seemed to notice the change in him. "What's wrong?"

He checked the mirrors again before answering her, but the truck was still there keeping pace. "We're being followed."

Her eyes widened in surprise before she turned and looked through the back window. "Are you sure?"

In the rearview mirror, he saw Kelsey turn too and look out the back. She'd obviously been paying more attention than he'd believed. "That car has stayed with us through several turns. I'm taking the long way and it's stayed with us."

Isabelle frowned. "What do we do?"

"Call for backup." He reached for his radio but before

he could place the call, the truck sped up, finally closing the distance between them. Drake dropped the radio and grabbed the steering wheel with both hands as the truck barreled toward them and rammed the back fender.

Kelsey screamed as the car hit them and Isabelle turned to reassure her. "We're going to be okay." Her tone didn't sound very certain.

Drake hit the accelerator as the truck sped up again and tried to come around them. If the other driver managed to get beside them, he could run them off the road, which Drake was certain was the goal. He wasn't giving up. "Isabelle, grab the radio and call for backup."

She reached to the floorboard and grabbed the hand link but the truck rammed them again and it slipped from her hands.

Drake pushed back against the truck but it was bigger and more powerful. "Hang on," he told them both then turned the wheel and rammed the truck. It easily took the blow without the driver losing control for even a second. He tried speeding up to outrun them but that didn't work either. He hit the sirens in case the driver didn't realize he was messing with a sheriff's deputy.

Apparently, they didn't care.

Isabelle scrambled for the handheld mic and pushed the button. "Help us. We need help."

The truck rammed them again on the side, causing the front end to spin out of control. They slid off the road, tumbling down the embankment. Screams rang in his ears as Isabelle and Kelsey cried out. He wanted to do something but it was now out of his hands.

As the car slammed to a stop, he was jerked forward, his seat belt caught and his head slammed against the headrest. He heard the sounds of the girls crying out then the hiss of metal crunching and car fluids releasing.

He struggled to glance to his side and saw Isabelle unconscious in the seat beside him, but before he could turn to check on Kelsey, darkness pulled him under.

SEVEN

Isabelle's head was pounding and her ears were still ringing as she slowly regained consciousness. She groaned as she tried to move but her body protested.

"Mom, Mom, are you okay?" Kelsey's voice was barely above a whisper but it was so full of fear that it grabbed Isabelle and pulled her back to consciousness.

She felt her daughter's hand on her shoulder but when she turned, the girl was standing hunched over. The vehicle was upside down and Kelsey was standing on the overturned roof while Isabelle was hanging in the air thanks to the seat belt. She reached for Kelsey's hand. "I'm okay. How about you?"

"I'm fine. You and Deputy Shaw both were knocked out and I was so worried."

Isabelle unbuckled her seat belt, dropping down to hit the roof of the vehicle, now the floor. She immediately gave Kelsey the once-over. Her hair was mussed and her eyes red from crying but otherwise she seemed okay.

She wasn't sure she could say the same for Drake. He too was buckled into his seat, which was now upside down. Blood dripped from a cut on his arm. She tapped his cheek, trying to revive him. "Drake, can you hear me? Drake, wake up."

It was no use. He wasn't moving. A quick check of his pulse and the gentle rise and fall of his chest told her he was still alive, but there was no telling when he might wake, and she knew they had no time to waste. They needed to get out of there quickly. "Kelsey, help me get him down." Kelsey got on one side while she took the other. She pressed the seat belt release and he tumbled down, with them doing their best to break his fall. The impact didn't even seem to faze him.

"Find the radio," she instructed Kelsey. "We need to call for help."

She scrambled until she found the mic on the floor. "Here it is."

She tried pressing the button, but nothing happened. She messed with the radio mounted to the dash. Still nothing.

"I don't think it's working, Mom."

Apparently, it had been damaged in the crash. She hoped the message she'd broadcast before they'd been run off the road had gone through. Otherwise, they were on their own until someone came looking for them. She had no doubt that when they didn't arrive at the court-house as planned, the deputies would try to find them. But would they come in time?

A crunch of leaves grabbed both her and Kelsey's at-tention. Kelsey turned to her, wide-eyed. "It's him," she whispered. "It's the man who ran us off the road."

Isabelle's heart raced at that prospect but she tried to keep her calm. "We don't know that. It might be help coming."

Kelsey leaned down so she could see outside the car then jumped back up and grabbed Isabelle. "Someone's coming."

Her daughter was trembling with fear, which caused Isabelle to go into mama bear mode. She'd come here to prevent any harm from coming to her daughter. She was going to protect her now from whomever was approaching them.

She knew Drake had weapons in the compartment in the back but it was locked. She reached for the key from the ignition and handed it to Kelsey. "See if you can unlock Drake's gear and find a gun." Kelsey hurried to the back, but her hands were shaking so much that Isabelle wasn't sure she could insert the key properly to make it work.

She spotted Drake's handgun still in its holster and reached for it. It was heavy in her hands but she would use it if necessary.

"Get behind me," she instructed her daughter, who dropped the keys then hurried back. She quivered behind her.

Lord, please help us out of this mess.

Tears pressed against Isabelle's eyes and she wished for Drake to wake up and take over. He would know how to keep them safe, but with him out of commission, she had no choice but to do it on her own.

"I've got a gun," she yelled at whoever was out there. "Come any closer and I will shoot you."

The footsteps stopped, and she knew for certain the person approaching had ill intentions. She held up the gun and waited. It was only a few moments before the steps began again.

Kelsey fell to the ground beside Drake, and the fear flowing off her was enough to strengthen Isabelle. She steadied the gun then fell to her knees for a better look at who was coming. She got down on her belly and spotted two denim- and boot-clad legs moving toward them. From her vantage point, she also saw a gun in his hand.

She wasn't waiting around for him to get close enough to use it. She aimed as best she could and fired off several shots, stunned by the recoil. She cried out and dropped the gun, but the assailant didn't seem to notice that. He swore then took off running back up the embankment. Isabelle retrieved the gun again and fired off several more shots.

The gunshots seemed to rouse Drake, whose eyes fluttered open. He glanced around at them. "What's happening?"

She couldn't see the assailant any longer, but she heard the sound of a truck door opening and closing, then an engine revving and tires squealing as he roared away.

"We're going to be okay," she assured him. Although he seemed conscious, he still looked confused.

Moments later, sirens sounded and police lights lit up the sky. Relief flooded through her as she heard voices commanding someone to follow that truck then several pairs of footsteps hurrying down the embankment. "Drake, are you okay?" a voice asked.

Isabelle held on to the gun, not willing to let it go until she was certain it was help.

"Drake, it's Josh and Gordon. Are you hurt?"

She dropped the gun and called out to them. "Josh, it's Isabelle and Kelsey. Drake's hurt."

A figure reached them and leaned down to peek

through the broken back window. "Are you and Kelsey hurt?"

"No, we're fine. Just shaken up."

He nodded then moved to the next window. The glass had shattered in the crash. He reached his hand in and felt for a pulse on Drake, who had closed his eyes and drifted off again. Josh hollered for help. "Isabelle, can you and Kelsey crawl out of the car for me?"

She motioned for her daughter to go first and Kelsey climbed out through the window. Isabelle followed, with Josh helping steady her. "We got your message and came as soon as we could find you."

"Thank you."

Another deputy helped her up the embankment to where an ambulance was waiting. Two paramedics passed her on her way up as they headed down to check on Drake. Her anxiety kicked in, hoping he wasn't hurt badly.

Kelsey threw herself into Isabelle's embrace, and she walked with her daughter to the ambulance where another pair of paramedics looked them over.

She sat on the bumper, waiting and watching for movement, for some assurance that Drake was all right. She heard yelling from the brush, and several more deputies hurried down. Terrible things rushed through her mind the longer it took to bring him up.

What if he didn't awaken again? What if his injuries were worse than she'd thought? Could she get through this without him? Could she bear to lose him again?

The brush shuffled then two paramedics broke through with Drake, one on each side of him, helping him walk. He looked dazed and barely conscious but he was on his feet.

Isabelle jumped from the ambulance, unable to stop

herself from running to him and hugging him tightly. He gingerly wrapped one arm around her and held her close.

"I was so worried when you didn't wake up," she told him. The idea of losing him again was unbearable.

He stroked her hair and did his best to reassure her. "I'm okay. You and Kelsey?"

She nodded. "We're both fine."

"We should get you to the hospital," one of the paramedics told him and he nodded.

She reluctantly released him and watched as they loaded him onto a gurney and into the ambulance.

A weight had been lifted from her. She didn't know what she would have done if something had happened to Drake.

It was an unexpected emotion, one that threw her for a moment. She'd been so concerned with trying to figure out if Drake was really Rayland that she hadn't even noticed when she'd allowed herself to truly feel something for him. She cared about him...no matter who he was.

Drake jerked awake and realized he was in the hospital. He sighed then leaned back on the bed. Thoughts about Isabelle and Kelsey were forefront in his mind. He knew they hadn't been injured in the crash but he still wanted to see them.

He pushed himself up, cringing from the pain.

"Deputy Shaw, you need to lie back down," the nurse who walked in insisted when she spotted him trying to sit up. "Your body has had quite a shock."

Every inch of his body hurt but he couldn't pinpoint one thing that hurt worse than the others—except maybe his head, which was pounding like a drum. "I need to make a call to check on someone."

At that moment, Josh stepped into the room. "Drake, they're fine. Do what the nurse says."

"Isabelle. Kelsey."

"They're okay. They've been examined by the ER staff and given the all clear. They weren't hurt. In fact, they're mostly just worried about you."

He recalled the way Isabelle had clung to him and how good it had felt to hold her.

"You lost consciousness," the nurse stated. "We had to perform a CT scan to make sure there weren't any lasting effects from when you hit your head."

"And was there?"

"No. You'll be sore for a few days and you've got some cuts and bruises but you'll recover." That was good news. He didn't want to be away from Isabelle and Kelsey for very long.

"Where are they?"

Josh waited until the nurse left the room before he responded. "Back at the safe house. We didn't find any trackers on your SUV or in any of your cell phones so we believe the motel is still secure. We're still trying to figure out how he knew which road you would be on. I'll phone Isabelle and let her know your prognosis. She'll be glad. She's been worried about you."

He heard the lilt of curiosity in his friend's tone—everyone at the scene had seen her run to him—but didn't bother addressing it. "Did you find out anything on the truck that ran us off the road?"

"I've got Jana scouring through video feeds looking for it. We'll find this guy."

"How did they know we would be on that road, Josh?" It was an isolated stretch that circumvented the highway. No one should have known when or where they would be coming from.

"I'm not sure, but I've made arrangements to change the meeting location to a business suite and we'll do it tomorrow. I'll handle the security myself. No one besides me, the sheriff, plus a few on security detail will know the location."

"What about the prosecutorial team? Is it possible the leak came from them?"

"I haven't discounted that possibility. That's why they won't be getting the address from me until Isabelle is already inside."

There was still the chance of an attack on their way from the meeting back to the motel, but Drake was satisfied that Josh was doing everything he could to ensure Isabelle's safety. "Thanks for handling this yourself." There were few people he trusted more than Josh Knight. He and Gordon had become Drake's closest friends and confidants.

"Yeah, of course. We'll do everything we can to keep them safe."

He was hoping to be out of the hospital and back to work by then, but he knew, if he wasn't physically able, Josh would handle things. He trusted Josh Knight with his life, yet it was difficult for him to let go of control when it came to Isabelle and Kelsey. They were becoming so important to him so quickly that it surprised him. He wasn't—couldn't be—Isabelle's husband as she believed, yet he also couldn't explain how fast he'd become emotionally attached to these two. It was almost like his life was entangled with theirs.

He racked his brain for some sliver of memory that might include Isabelle or a life different from the one he'd known but there was nothing. Yes, he'd dreamed about her for years and he'd instinctively called her by a name only her husband had used, but those weren't things he actually remembered. He couldn't recall them at will or connect them to a specific time or place. His first real memory was of watching the small TV in his bedroom in Alabama and the excruciating pain of rehabilitation that had allowed him to walk again. He didn't even recall being in the hospital in New Orleans or how he'd gotten home. He hadn't questioned who he was when his sister called him Drake. He'd been confused at first, but then he'd settled into a routine and way of life that he didn't question.

Now he had questions and only one person he knew could provide the answers. His mother had passed away years ago. Only his sister remained of his family—and he'd been avoiding her call for weeks.

He picked up the phone and dialed the number for her. She sounded surprised when she answered but glad to hear from him. He got straight to the point. "Connie, can you meet me? We really need to talk."

The prosecutor closed her notebook as she leaned back in her seat. They'd been at it for a grueling six hours of testimony prep. She and her colleagues had lobbed mock questions at Isabelle in order to show her how to defend against the attacks they all knew would be coming from the defense attorneys at trial. Charles Jeffries had deep pockets and a team of the best defense lawyers in the state.

"I think you're ready," attorney Monica Sellers stated.

Isabelle took a deep, relieved breath. "What do we do now?"

"The trial starts in three days. You'll be one of the first witnesses after opening statements conclude. We'll arrange to fly you back to Memphis in a few days."

She shuddered at the thought of returning home and confronting Charles Jeffries. On the one hand, it would feel good to show him that his threats and attacks hadn't prevented her testimony. On the other, she had no desire to look into his greedy, power-hungry eyes.

They ran down the rest of the details then Josh arrived to walk her back to the SUV for the return ride home.

"Are you certain this is safe?" she asked him. She'd purposefully left Kelsey at the motel this time, just in case. Deputy Gordon had agreed to stay and watch her, and Isabelle had decided that would be better than bringing her out into the open.

"I've arranged to have two patrol cars follow us out of town. They'll stay alert to notice any cars that might be following us and they'll take care of them."

She was grateful he was being so dedicated with her safety. Drake had had nothing but good things to say about both Gordon and Josh, and if he trusted them then so did she. "Have you spoken to Drake?"

"I did. He's being released this afternoon. I'll swing by and pick him up later then bring him to the motel."

"Wouldn't he be more comfortable at home? Shouldn't he be resting?"

"He probably should but he won't be able to without seeing with his own eyes that you and your daughter are okay." She caught a slight smile as he made that comment and felt her face warm.

She wasn't embarrassed about her growing feelings for Drake Shaw, but it was a little awkward to know that everyone had seen the way she'd run to him after the wreck, putting her feelings on display. At least Josh seemed to imply that the feeling was mutual on Drake's part.

"How long have you known him?" Isabelle asked.

"Since he joined the force four years ago. He's a good man. He cares about people and has a heart for helping others. But he doesn't talk much about his past." He glanced her way before turning his eyes back to the road. "I suppose you know something about why, don't you?"

She definitely had her suspicions, which were every day feeling more and more like fact. "I might know something."

"I know you and your daughter will be heading back to Memphis once this trial is over. I just hope you don't go breaking his heart, ma'am."

She knew a thing or two about heartbreak. Although she had no intention of hurting Drake, she realized she hadn't intended to care for him either. And yet, they'd grown close very quickly. She needed to be cautious. The last time she'd put her heart out there on the line, it had been shattered. She still hadn't fully recovered from the loss.

"About that, Deputy. As you know the trial starts in a few days. The prosecutor wants me back in Tennessee in just a few days, but I'm still worried about the threats against me. I'm not comfortable allowing my daughter to return with me. I wonder, if it's possible, if she could remain here in Mercy, with you guarding her."

He gripped the steering wheel. "I'm sure Drake will be hap—"

"I want to ask Drake to come with me as kind of my bodyguard. I feel safer with him around. Only Kelsey needs to be protected too. Drake thinks a lot of you, Josh. I would consider it a favor if you would watch out for her while I'm away."

He considered that for a moment. "I'd have to clear it with the sheriff."

"I can ask her myself. It'll only be for a few days."

He nodded. "If Drake and the sheriff are okay with it then I'm willing. Gordon and I can rotate shifts and we can get an extension at the motel."

"Thank you. That would take a load off my mind."

"Have you spoken to Drake about going with you?"

"Not yet but I think he'll agree."

Josh smiled and nodded. "I'm sure he will."

"Do you have an issue with that, Deputy?"

His smile faded. "I'm not sure. He's my friend so I want him to be happy, but I guess I'm not ready to lose another good deputy. We recently had one of our best investigators move away."

"Mike Tyner. Yes, Drake told me about him."

"I was thrilled for him that he met someone but this was his home. He was born and raised here in Mercy. Drake has only been here a short while but he fits here." He looked at her and his face reddened. "Listen to me carrying on. I'm sorry. That's not very professional of me."

"No, it's fine. I can see how much you care for your friends. I like that. Also, the last thing I want to do is to hurt Drake. Far from it. I think we could be very happy together."

As they turned into the motel parking lot, she thought about how true the words were. She was convinced of Drake's true identity, but even if by some chance more proof emerged that he was in fact Drake Shaw and no one else, she could still see her falling for him.

In fact, in her heart, she'd already crossed that line.

He parked then got out and met with Deputy Gordon for several minutes. Isabelle went inside to find Kelsey munching on chips and watching reruns of *The Andy Griffith Show.*

"How was it?" she asked Isabelle.

"Exhausting," she admitted. "But I think I'm ready to face Jeffries in court. The trial starts in three days."

"Good," Kelsey stated. "Because I'm ready to get out of this place and back to my life. My friends are not going to believe what I've been through when I tell them."

Isabelle grimaced at her daughter's words. She'd thought her exhausting day was over but it was only just beginning. She patted the bed beside her. "Come sit with me for a minute, Kel. I need to tell you something."

Her daughter was not going to be pleased with the new arrangements she'd just made.

The doctor had ordered a twenty-four-hour observation since Drake had lost consciousness in the crash. He'd protested and assured everyone he was fine but Sheriff Thompson had insisted he remain in the hospital for the duration. That had been the end of it. He'd been stuck in this hospital room for the past day. Now, at last, his discharge time had arrived and he was antsy to get out and get back to Isabelle.

The nurse walked in with his papers. "Here you go,

Deputy." She gave his bandages one last check. "Everything looks good."

Josh entered as she was leaving and Drake was glad to see him. "About time," he grumbled at his friend who only laughed.

"I was busy making sure Isabelle got back and forth to her meeting with the prosecutor."

"How did it go?"

"Everything went fine. She did her trial prep and now she's back at the motel with her daughter and Gordon."

Drake slipped into his shoes and tied the laces. "Take me to her."

"First things first. We need to check in with the sheriff."

Drake inwardly groaned at being kept away from Isabelle longer, but Josh was right about needing to confer with the sheriff.

When they reached the sheriff's office, several people called out to him and asked how he was doing. He thanked them for their concern and assured everyone he was fine. It was good to have coworkers who were more like family. This was the first place he'd truly felt he belonged... at least that he could remember.

He'd convinced himself that the loss of those memories of the first twenty-five years of his life was no great tragedy. Not when he had his mom and sister to fill in the gaps. After meeting Isabelle though, he was questioning everything.

Sheriff Thompson met him and Josh in the conference room. She eyed Drake as she sat down. "How are you feeling?"

"I'm good," he assured her, already tired of repeating that line. "I'm ready to get back to work."

"He's still moving a little slowly," Josh added, and Drake shot him a side-eyed angry look.

"My body is a little stiff but it'll work itself out," he countered.

Sheriff Thompson looked ready to bench him, which was the last thing he wanted. Getting back to Isabelle was all he'd been able to think of since the crash. "Josh and Gordon seem to be handling the protection detail fine if you need another day or two to recuperate," the sheriff suggested.

"I don't. I'm good now."

"Still, I'd feel better if Josh and Gordon remained for a few days more until you're back at one hundred percent."

He didn't argue with that. In fact, he was glad of it knowing that he was going to have to leave to go meet his sister tomorrow.

"It's only three more days until the trial begins, then our part in all of this is over." As much as Drake was looking forward to the danger to Isabelle and Kelsey coming to end, the thought of her leaving town for good made his stomach sink.

"Actually, it's not," Josh interrupted. Drake turned and looked at him, confused. "Earlier when I was driving Isabelle back to the motel, she said she wanted to leave her daughter here until after she gave her testimony at trial. She was worried about the girl's safety."

Drake turned to look at Sheriff Thompson for her reaction, only Josh wasn't finished dropping news.

"She also had another request. She wants Drake to go with her to Memphis and stay with her during the trial."

Sheriff Thompson's lips pressed together, and Drake could nearly see the *no* about to roll from her lips.

Knowing that Isabelle wanted him with her reinforced his resolve. "I'm doing it," he told them both.

"That's way out of our jurisdiction," Sheriff Thompson reminded him.

"Then I won't go officially. Call it vacation time or whatever, but I'm going."

He stared at her, praying she wouldn't try to talk him out of this. Isabelle's safety had become his first concern and the threats against her would only increase until she took the witness stand.

Finally, Sheriff Thompson conceded. "Fine, but you'll be at the mercy of the local police. As for the girl, we'll continue our stay at the motel, but I'll be assigning a female deputy to stay with her as well while her mother is gone." She stood to leave but stopped and turned back to Drake. "You have to know this protection detail cannot go on forever. I can't justify that. You're going to have to accept that their time in Mercy is coming to an end."

She walked out and Drake stood to go. He was anxious to get back to them. Their time in Mercy might be coming to an end, but he wasn't yet ready to end their time together. And he wasn't about to let Isabelle face Charles Jeffries all on her own.

Kelsey had eaten then fallen asleep with her earbuds in. She was happy to have her phone back so she could listen to her music, but she still wasn't happy about being cooped up at the motel and unable to talk to her friends.

Isabelle felt her frustration but they had to be smart.

Still, the mundane existence of watching generic television was grating on her nerves as well.

She stood to turn off the TV and saw headlights of a vehicle pulling into a parking spot in front of the room. The adjoining door opened and Deputy Gordon stuck his head in. "It's Josh returning with Drake," he told her before she could worry about the new arrival.

She hurried through the adjoining room, watching as Gordon opened the door, revealing the sight of Drake exiting the SUV. Isabelle ran to him and hugged him and he pulled her into his embrace.

"I'm okay," he assured her. He pulled away so he could look at her and touch her cheek. "You and Kelsey?"

"We're fine." This was the first time she'd seen him since the wreck. Josh and Gordon both had assured her that Drake was fine and she'd even spoken to him on the phone, but seeing him, touching him, was the only way she could know for certain he wasn't seriously hurt.

She saw him glance behind her and turned to see Kelsey standing in the doorway.

"Hey, Kelsey," Drake said.

"Are you okay?" she asked, and Isabelle could see the worry in the lines in her eyes.

He was quick to reassure her too. "I'm a little sore but otherwise I'm fine."

"Good." She gave him a small smile then turned and walked back into the room.

"She may not show it much but she was worried about you," Isabelle told him. Her daughter, while friendly and outgoing, didn't get attached to people very quickly, especially adults. Her friend Tracy had won her over slowly, over the course of months. But Isabelle could see she'd formed a liking for Drake too, despite only knowing him for a short time, and she was glad.

Josh cleared his throat to pull their attention away from one another. "We stopped and got food." He pulled several bags and a tray of drinks from the back seat.

Gordon took the tray. "Let me help you with that." He glanced at Isabelle and Drake then turned back to Josh. "Let's go back inside and give these two a few minutes to catch up."

Josh followed him inside then closed the door, leaving Isabelle and Drake standing alone in the parking lot. She was still in his arms and she didn't even care.

"Feel like taking a walk with me?" he asked her.

"Do you think it's safe?"

"I think it is. As far as we know, the motel is secure. No one knows we're here. Besides, we won't stay out for long," he assured her. "We'll stay by the pool."

She agreed, glad for the opportunity to stretch her legs and also for the alone time with him. The pool was only steps outside the door of their room, so she could still keep an eye on it.

Drake slipped his hand into hers, and it felt so natural to lean into him as they walked. The bright moon made even a motel swimming area seem romantic.

"I was so worried about you and Kelsey. I couldn't think of anything else except getting out of that hospital and getting back to you."

"I know what you mean. The last time I saw you, you were barely able to stand. I wanted to go sit with you and let you know I was there but I couldn't." Tears welled in her eyes at how out of control her life had become. "Have they found the man who ran us off the road?"

His jaw tightened. "No. He's managed to stay off the sheriff's office radar, which makes me believe he must be a professional."

She shuddered at the thought. It was bad enough that Jeffries had hired someone to come after her but a professional hitman? She'd had no idea how ruthless he could be.

"Josh told me about your request that I go with you back to Memphis for the trial."

She held her breath, worried that she'd overstepped by mentioning it to Josh before she'd even asked Drake.

"The sheriff gave the okay. Josh and Gordon along with a female deputy will keep Kelsey here at the motel. I'll be there with you, Isabelle, every day until this ordeal is over."

She stopped walking and leaned into his arms. He pulled her close and it felt right. She didn't care if he was Drake Shaw or Rayland Morris. Whatever his name was, he was the man she was falling in love with. He'd become so important to her.

He lifted her face to him then lowered his face to hers, hesitating before their lips met. She wasn't going to allow hesitation to stop what they both wanted, so she raised herself and met his mouth. His arms tightened around her and she lost herself in the moment. Everything that had gone wrong with her and Ray seemed to evaporate along with the guilt and regrets. This wasn't a reunion as much as it was a new beginning.

He ended the kiss then stroked her cheek with his finger, awe shining in his eyes as he stared at her and his voice full of choked back emotion.

"I feel like I belong with you," he whispered in her ear, and she clung to him.

"You do," she told him.

"I called my sister. I'm meeting her at a diner to talk to her about all of this."

She blew out a breath and steadied herself. She was glad he was finally moving away from his insistence that he couldn't be Rayland. She had no idea what his sister would have to say about the matter but Isabelle was glad he was reaching out. Maybe now he could finally put to rest the doubts about himself. She also wanted answers about how this terrible situation had occurred and why she'd been denied her husband all these years. But most of all, she wanted another chance at love.

"Tell me about him," Drake asked, surprising her. She'd spent so much time thinking about the implosion of their marriage and the guilt she'd carried. She smiled now, remembering the best of the man she'd fallen in love with all those years ago.

"Twelfth grade chemistry. He smiled at me from across the classroom, and I just knew he was looking at someone behind me so I completely ignored him. After class, he approached me and asked me to help him study for an upcoming quiz. I agreed of course because I was good at chemistry and he was Ray Morris, the most popular boy in school, while I was nerdy and shy."

Drake laughed. "I doubt that."

"It's true. I didn't even know that Ray knew I even existed. He was handsome and charismatic and an athlete and everyone's friend. But he was also very kind and reached out to others unexpectedly as he did with me. The quiz of course was just an excuse to get me alone and get to know me better. I discovered later on that he actually had the highest grade point average in that class and didn't need my tutoring."

Drake smiled at her retelling. "Sounds like love to me."

"It was. I fell for him hard and, incredibly enough, he loved me back." Tears slipped down her cheek but she didn't bother to wipe them away. They were good tears. "He was an only child and very close to his parents. He worked with his father at his construction company and loved the job. When they were killed in a car wreck a few years after we were married, I think it broke something in him. He shut down. He couldn't handle the weight of his grief and the responsibilities he'd inherited. It ended up driving a wedge between us."

He turned to her. "I'm so sorry, Izzy."

"No, you don't have to apologize. I'm the one who…" Her chin quivered as she gathered her courage to confess her shame. "I told him that I didn't want to be married to him anymore. I asked him to leave. That's why he was there in New Orleans and not at home with us. He called me every week telling me how much he missed us and how he'd straightened his life up and realized what he was missing. The last time he called, he asked to come home, and I told him no. His final words to me were about how much he loved me and how he was going to fight for our marriage. I just blew him off. I was so angry and heartbroken at all the things that had gone wrong between us that I couldn't remember how much we'd once meant to one another. Then, I got the call about the explosion and the news that he wasn't coming home and I knew it was because of me. He would have been home if it wasn't for me. I'm so sorry."

The tears she'd been repressing exploded in her. He

pulled her into his arms and held her tightly as she sobbed into his shoulder.

"You don't have to be sorry either." He held her face in his hands and his eyes scoured hers. "I wish I could tell you what he was thinking and feeling but I'm sure it was about you, about getting back to you." He stared into her eyes then pushed a strand of hair from her face and kissed her cheek and forehead before finding her lips. "I'm not surprised he singled you out that day in class, Izzy. You don't seem to know just how amazing you really are."

She didn't tell him so but that was something Ray had told her countless times. She clung to him, not ever wanting to let him go again, not even to meet with his sister tomorrow. But he had to go. It was time to put this question to rest once and for all.

"When will you meet with Connie?"

"Tomorrow morning. I'll be back after lunch. Josh and Gordon will still be here. If you or Kelsey need anything, let them know and they'll take care of it. I trust them both."

As they reached the motel room, she lingered for only a moment with her hand in his before kissing him softly. "Hurry back," she whispered before opening the door and stepping inside. She saw his shadow pass by the window then heard the door to the next room open and close.

Isabelle stretched out on the bed, still basking in the memory of their kiss and all the past problems she'd finally admitted to. She'd always wanted him to know how sorry she was for her actions and she'd finally gotten that chance.

"It's not fair," Kelsey mumbled. It was only at that moment that she realized the girl was watching her.

She sat up and Kelsey frowned. "Have you been crying?"

She nodded and reached for a tissue to wipe her eyes. "Yes, but it's okay. They're good tears. What's not fair?"

"That you get to be with your boyfriend but I can't even talk to Adam."

"Kelsey, don't be silly. Drake isn't my boyfriend."

She lifted her head from the pillow. "But you like him, don't you?"

She touched her lips, recalling their kiss. "I guess I do." She hadn't shared her beliefs about Drake being her husband with Kelsey. Her daughter didn't seem to have noticed the resemblance—probably because she'd been so young when he'd died. "What about you? Do you like him?"

She shrugged. "I guess he's okay. I don't like that he's so strict."

"He's not being strict, Kelsey. He's being protective. It's his job."

Kelsey gave a loud moan of frustration instead of responding, obviously realizing this line of discussion was a losing argument.

Isabelle sighed and didn't press the matter. At some point, she was going to have to explain to Kelsey the truth about what was going on and who Drake was, but she wasn't going to broach that topic tonight. Maybe tomorrow after Drake's conversation with his sister, they would have more answers and she could tell Kelsey the truth with certainty…that Drake Shaw was actually her father.

EIGHT

He sat in his car staring at the front of the diner and contemplating whether or not to get out. He was more anxious about this meeting than he'd thought he would be. He'd been the one to call and ask her to meet, but now that he was here, he was hesitating. This meeting could either reaffirm what he'd always believed and put to rest his doubts about his own identity or upend his life completely. Either way, he couldn't keep wondering. No matter what his feelings for Isabelle, he was owed the truth for them both. He took a deep breath to bolster his confidence then got out of the car and walked into the diner.

His sister was seated at a booth in the corner. She smiled as she caught his attention then waved. He walked over, leaned down to kiss her cheek in greeting, then slid into the booth opposite her.

"You look good, Connie." And she did.

In fact, she looked better than he'd seen her in years. The weight of the burdens she'd been carrying around for most of her life seemed to have faded and a newfound freedom showed on her face and in her manner.

"I'm glad you called," she said. "It's been too long."

But then she noticed the bandages and frowned. "Are you hurt? What happened?"

"It was a car wreck. Someone ran me off the road but I'm not seriously hurt."

"You should be resting. We could have gotten together another time."

He shook his head. It had to be now. "This couldn't wait. Connie, I want to ask you about the accident at the refinery."

Her face paled. Her unburdened demeanor vanished. "Really, Drake, haven't we moved past that?"

"I'm not sure I ever did. You know that I never recovered any memories from the accident or of my life before it happened."

She nodded. "I'm aware."

"I recently met someone, Connie, and meeting her has made me start wondering about who I really am."

"What does that mean, Drake?"

"For years, I've been dreaming about a woman and a little girl with blond pigtails. A week ago, I met that woman and her daughter."

She gave him a bewildered smile. "What do you mean you met a woman from your dreams?"

"I started sketching this woman in my journal before I'd even met her." He pulled the journal from his jacket pocket and opened it to the page where he'd sketched Isabelle. He'd brought it with him to show her he wasn't making this up. "I've dreamed about her for years and didn't know why or who she was. Now I know she's a real person."

She stared at the drawings and looked confused. "How is that possible?"

He opened his cell phone and showed her the photo of Rayland Morris. "I looked up the accident at the refinery online. Eight men died that day, including this man, Rayland Morris." She stared at the photo on the screen and her face fell. "He had a wife and a five-year-old daughter." He tapped the drawing. "At the time he died, they looked like this."

She slid the phone across the table back to him and lowered her eyes. "Are you saying you remember her?"

"No, not a memory, not really. That part of my life is still blank. But I can't deny there is something familiar about her. I'm drawn to her. Plus, the drawings. They must have come from someplace deep inside me. It's obvious I've met her before. How else do you explain the dreams?"

"And what does she believe?"

"She buried a burned body. She never questioned her husband's death...not until we met. Now she's sure I'm him. I don't even know how that's possible."

Her face hardened. She folded her arms protectively across her chest as she stared at him. "Is this why you wanted to see me? I don't know what you want me to say."

He sighed and rubbed his face. "I'm sorry. I don't know what I want you to say either." He knew this was a difficult topic for her, for them both, but he pressed on. "You were the one who identified me at the hospital, weren't you?"

She fingered her coffee cup then nodded yes.

He took a deep breath. He just had to summon up the courage to ask her the question he really wanted to know. "Did you ever have any doubts? Ever thought that maybe you'd identified the wrong person?"

He'd expected an emphatic "no" but it didn't come.

Instead, she poured creamer into her coffee then picked up her spoon and stirred it. He knew her well enough to know she wasn't shutting him out but carefully considering her response.

And he didn't even know he was holding his breath for her answer until her response gut punched him.

"Not at first I didn't."

He leaned back in his chair and rubbed a hand through his hair, dumbfounded by the implication. "What do you mean by 'not at first'?"

"You have to understand how frantic I was when I got the call about the explosion. Mama was still listed as your emergency contact, but she was so sick from the cancer treatments that she couldn't go. I made the hour-long drive, all the time praying that you were okay and I would get there in time."

"And when you arrived?"

"The doctors led me into a hospital room. You were laying on the bed and what I could see of your face was covered in bandages. They told me you were badly burned. At first, I wasn't sure but you were the right build as my brother and had the same dark hair. Then the policeman who was there showed me some belongings they said you had on you at the time of the explosion—what was left of a jacket and a leather wallet I gave you for Christmas one year with your initials. They wanted me to confirm you were my brother and I had no reason to believe you weren't."

He leaned back as he soaked in her story. If he wasn't Drake then why had he had those belongings on him? "But you had doubts?"

"Not at first. As the weeks went by and you started recuperating, I did notice some different mannerisms and your voice seemed different, but it was easy to chalk it up to the trauma of the explosion and your injuries. Whenever I wondered, I thought about Mama. She was so sick, Drake. I kept telling myself on the way to New Orleans that night that learning you'd died in an explosion would surely kill her. I couldn't lose you both so I guess I did my best to ignore the differences. Only, the more you healed, the more noticeable they became. There were so many mornings when I kept expecting you to look at me and tell me that you weren't Drake—that you were someone else completely. Only, you never did. You never remembered any differently."

He had a moment of pity for the predicament his sister had been in but it quickly faded into anger at what had been stolen from him. "You never told me I might have been someone other than your brother."

"Because I didn't know for sure." A tear slid down her cheek. "Truthfully, I didn't *want* to know," she confessed. "When we were kids, we were always close. We were all each other had. Mama worked all the time and it was just me and Drake. But I never felt that connection after the explosion."

He hadn't either. In fact, he'd always felt like he didn't belong, like he'd been a visitor in his own life. He leaned his arm on the table and put his head in his hand as all the evidence seemed to come together. The resemblance, the hobbies, the dreams of Isabelle and Kelsey, the nickname. Everything clicked into place. He looked at his sister. "Connie, I think I'm him. I think I'm Rayland Morris."

She shook her head, still refusing to acknowledge it. "How do you explain that you had Drake's jacket?"

"I can't." But that didn't make him Drake Shaw. "Maybe I got cold and he loaned it to me. You said all the identifying information was burned. I still don't know how or why it happened but every day I'm more convinced that a terrible mistake was made."

She still shook her head. "No, the photographs of us when we were kids. It's you. It's you, Drake."

He shook his head. He and the man who died that night ten years ago had certainly favored each other but he realized now that everyone who'd identified him had all only seen what they'd expected to see. As she'd said earlier, they'd all ignored the differences out of love or ignorance or whatever reasoning they'd needed to make sense of life.

She wiped away a tear. "I don't want to lose my brother."

"I think you already did." He didn't say that to be mean but believed it was true. Drake Shaw had died years ago.

Yet, he and Connie still shared a history even if it didn't extend all the way back to childhood. He reached across the table and held her hand. "I'm sorry we weren't closer. You've always been good to me and taken care of me. I love you and I didn't come here to hurt you, Connie."

She nodded. "I know, I know. This is my fault. I made a mistake because I refused to see the truth."

He couldn't blame her for the choices she'd made during such a turbulent time, and he knew her well enough to believe she would have never purposefully kept him from his true family. She'd done the best she could in a tough situation.

Part of him had come here expecting her to fight the truth, to insist that she knew her brother and it was him.

Now, her confession that she might have made a mistake in identifying him was hitting him hard.

The last ten years of his life had been a lie. He'd been living another man's life. It made sense why he hadn't felt like he'd belonged anywhere in Drake Shaw's life.

He wasn't Drake Shaw at all.

He was Rayland Morris...and Isabelle's husband.

Isabelle opened a bottle of pain reliever. Her head was pulsing and she knew from experience that a migraine was inching forward. She needed to stem it off before she was down for days with it. She couldn't afford that to happen now, of all times.

Kelsey approached her timidly, which instinctively told her she wanted something and was afraid to bring it up.

Isabelle sighed. She didn't have time for teenage games. "What is it, Kelsey?"

"Adam's family barbecue is today. You said you'd think about letting me go."

Isabelle stared at her daughter dumbfounded. That invitation seemed like it had been made eons ago, even if it had only been a few days. But, after all that had happened, what could Kelsey be thinking? "Absolutely not. It's not safe for you or for them."

"I will be safe, Mama. I promise."

"You can't make that kind of promise, Kelsey. Someone is after us, following our every move. They've already tried to grab you once. Plus, do you realize the danger you'd be putting Adam and his family into?"

"Shouldn't they get to decide whether they're willing to take that risk or not? Shouldn't *I* get to make some decisions about my own life?" Kelsey folded her arms defiantly. "Ever since you agreed to testify against your boss, my life has been a nightmare. Why did you have to do this? Why can't you just stop?"

"It's too late for that, honey. I don't even know who it is that's coming after us."

"It has to be Mr. Jeffries." She walked over to the motel's phone on the nightstand and held the receiver out to her. "Please just call him and tell him you'll back off."

Isabelle wanted to give Kelsey back the life that had been stolen from her. But she couldn't agree not to testify, especially now. There was no going back.

"Kelsey, I'm sorry but it's not going to happen."

A knock on the adjoining door alerted her that Drake had returned. He opened it and stuck his head in. "Everything okay in here?"

"We're fine," Isabelle tried to reassure him, but when she turned back to Kelsey, she was fuming.

Her daughter crossed her arms and her face turned hard. "I hate this," she screamed. "I hate you! I've lost everything. My friends, my school. Now I finally made new friends and I can't be around them either."

Drake pushed through into the room. "Kelsey, this is not your mother's fault. I realize—"

"This is none of your business," she screamed, cutting him off. "You're not my father and you can't tell me what to do." She turned on her heel and ran into the bathroom, slamming the door hard enough to shake the room.

Isabelle headed for the bathroom door but Drake took her arm to stop her. "She just needs some time to calm down," he told her. "She's been through a lot. It's understandable she's upset."

"She shouldn't have spoken to you that way. She

shouldn't have said what she did about you not being her father."

He turned away and shoved his hands into his pockets. She could see that had stung him. "She's not wrong. She hasn't had a father be there for her since she was five years old."

"Drake, that's not your fault. It's nobody's fault. It's just the way it is."

"Blame has nothing to do with this, Izzy. It's the truth. Kelsey grew up without a father. I can't change that. Neither can you." He rubbed his face. "I've always wanted to feel like a part of a family. Turns out, I was part of one all along."

That sounded to her like he was admitting what she'd already surmised. "Did you speak with your sister?"

He nodded. "She agreed that there might have been a misidentification. It is possible that I'm him, Izzy. Your husband. Kelsey's father. That should make me happy but then I look at Kelsey and see how angry she is."

"That has nothing to do with you. It's all about me. You have to stop beating yourself up over this, Drake. I don't know why God allowed this to happen but He's been there for me and Kelsey, providing for us, guiding us." She touched his arm and he turned to look at her. "He even guided us to the cabin, to Mercy…to find you."

He pulled her into his embrace and she leaned in. It felt so good to be held by him. She stared up into his face, so familiar yet so different from the man she'd married. He'd not only grown older but much more handsome. His eyes lingered on her lips and she knew he wanted to kiss her. She wanted that too, only he was holding back.

She leaned up and pressed her lips against his, giving

him the okay. He responded by wrapping his arms around and her pulling her tightly against him as the kiss deepened. It was so familiar, yet new and exciting as well. The years spent apart seemed to melt away.

He touched her hair and emotion cracked his voice. "I missed you, Izzy. Even when I couldn't remember you, I missed you."

She knew that was true. He'd dreamed about her and Kelsey. Somehow, his unconscious mind had fought to get back to them. She leaned into his embrace. At least something good had come from this nightmare.

"I should go get Kelsey. She needs to apologize. We should also talk to her about who you really are."

She walked to the bathroom door, already working out in her mind how she was going to break the news to Kelsey that her dad was alive. It would be a shock but, as she'd thought before, maybe this was all a blessing in disguise.

She tried to open the door but it was locked from inside. Isabelle knocked but there was no answer. "Kelsey, it's Mom. Open the door. I need to talk to you."

Still no response.

"She's not responding," she told Drake.

He tried the knob and knocked himself, calling out to Kelsey and getting only silence back. "Stand back from the door. I'm going to break it down."

Isabelle backed away as he kicked at the knob. The lock broke and the door swung open. They both glanced into the tiny bathroom, but Kelsey was nowhere in sight. Isabelle's heart sank at the sight of the open window. "She must have crawled out."

Drake called for Gordon, who appeared at the doorway of the adjoining room.

"Kelsey went out the window," he told him and they both leaped into action. "Stay here," Drake told Isabelle before rushing through the door with Gordon to search for her daughter.

Isabelle chewed on her fingernail in frustration. Kelsey's attitude had grown worse and worse over the past few days, but she'd never expected her daughter to sneak out. Especially when they were under protective guard.

Given how angry she was about missing the barbecue, Isabelle knew exactly where she'd run to. She pulled out her cell phone and dialed Kelsey's cell phone. It immediately went to voicemail before she remembered the service wasn't active. Drake had returned Kelsey's phone to her but only after removing the SIM card. She couldn't make or accept calls. The location indicator had also been turned off so Isabelle couldn't track Kelsey's phone either. However, she still had Adam's phone number. Surely Kelsey would be in touch with him when she could.

He didn't answer either, but this time she left a voicemail. "Adam, it's Mrs. Morris. Is Kelsey with you? Please have her call me as soon as possible. It's urgent." She left her number even though she knew it showed up on his phone.

The door opened and Drake hurried back inside. Isabelle was disappointed to see Kelsey wasn't with him. "We searched the parking lot and the pool and laundry areas but didn't find her. Gordon's gone to the office to get a passkey so we can check the empty rooms."

"How would she have gotten into one of them?"

He shrugged. "An unlocked door or open window.

We'll sweep the outside to see if we find any broken glass. She couldn't have gotten far."

"She's angry about not being able to go to a barbecue with Adam. She'll probably be trying to contact him. I tried calling his cell phone but it went to voicemail."

"I'll try too, and I'll call Josh and have him track down Adam's parents so they can be on the lookout."

"How could she get to their house? And he doesn't even know where she is."

The frown on his face told her he was already thinking ahead. His tone was apologetic as he explained. "If she manages to walk to the highway, she could hitch a ride."

"No." Isabelle's knees buckled at the thought of her daughter accepting a ride from a perfect stranger.

Drake was quick to help her sit on the bed. "That's just one possibility," he reminded her. "More than likely, she's still on the property sulking somewhere."

"How could she be so reckless?" Her daughter didn't seem to comprehend the danger they were in.

"If we don't find her soon, we'll call in backup from the sheriff's office to help search the woods and the highway."

"I'll help search."

He pressed on her shoulders. "I'd rather you stay here. She may return on her own and we need to know if she does."

She pushed past his hold and stood to face him. "She's my daughter. She might come when I call to her."

"You're the one she's mad at, remember?" Drake pointed out. "Please, Isabelle, just let us do our jobs. I can't concentrate on finding Kelsey if I'm worried about you too."

She saw the stress on his face over this situation.

"I'm asking you to trust me," he said. As much as she didn't want to just sit and wait, she *did* trust him.

She gave him a clipped nod of her head. "Okay."

He walked to the door but turned back to her before he left. "Lock this and don't open it for anyone except me, Gordon or Kelsey."

She did as he instructed. The bathroom door still stood open, and she prayed Kelsey would climb back through it and apologize but that seemed unlikely. She tried Adam's number again and, again, it went to voicemail.

She shuddered at the thought of Kelsey making it to the highway and hitchhiking. That was horrible enough to think about when they didn't have a maniac trying to kill them.

Isabelle paced the motel room for what seemed like hours before a knock at the door had her running to it. She peeked through the curtain and saw Drake. She quickly unlocked the door and swung it open.

Her heart sank to see him alone. "You didn't find her?"

His face said it all. "We've searched all the rooms and places where she might be hiding. Gordon is speaking with Sheriff Thompson about getting a crew together to widen the search."

"What about Adam?"

"I had a patrol car go to his house. He's not there and he's not answering their calls either. His parents don't have the ability to track his cell, but they've given us permission to contact the carrier to do so. They're also contacting the company that monitors the GPS in his car. Someone will call me when they know something more." He touched her arm. "They do think he got a call from Kelsey before he left."

Her mind was spinning. "But how?"

"We don't know yet but we're still searching. It's possible she called him to come pick her up."

His cell phone rang and he grabbed it and placed it on speaker. "Yeah, what do you have?" he asked the deputy calling.

"The Burches tracked Adam's car to the lake. According to his GPS, it's parked in the public lot."

Isabelle's heart soared. "The lake! They went back to the cabin. They must have," she realized. Only as quickly as her realization had come, the fear slammed into her. "Drake, if that man who attacked us is watching the cabin—"

"We're headed there now," Drake insisted.

"I'll meet you there," the deputy stated.

"No," Drake told him. "You stay there with the Burches until we know what's happening. I've got this."

He ended the call and looked down at Isabelle with a look of concern. "I don't suppose I could convince you to remain here, could I?"

She stood to face him. "Not a chance."

Her cell phone rang and she saw it was Adam calling. Relief flooded her. "Adam, is Kelsey with you? Where are you?"

His garbled tone immediately put her on edge. "She was." He groaned in pain. "Someone jumped us. He knocked me out. I just came to and saw the multiple missed calls on my cell."

Fear raced through Isabelle and her hands shook. "What do you mean? Where is she?"

She heard him calling Kelsey's name with no reply and her heart sank. "She's gone."

Drake grabbed the phone. "Adam, where are you?"

"Down by the lake not far from the cabin. Kelsey called me and asked me to pick her up."

"We're on the way."

Drake grabbed her hand and they jumped into his car. He turned on the sirens as he maneuvered to the cabin.

Isabelle concentrated on her breathing. It was all she could do to keep herself from becoming hysterical. Where was her daughter?

Drake turned into the public lot and screeched to a halt beside Adam's car. They jumped out and ran down to the beach, finding Adam sitting on the grass, holding his head in his hands. He was sporting a busted lip and a bruise on his forehead.

Isabelle ran to him. "Are you okay?"

"Tell us what happened," Drake commanded.

"We were walking to my car when a man ran up and grabbed Kelsey. I tried to fight him off but he hit me." Tears filled his eyes as he struggled to finish. "She was screaming when I lost consciousness. The next thing I knew, I woke up and she was gone."

Drake stood just in time to catch Isabelle as her knees buckled. She couldn't comprehend what was happening.

Her daughter was gone, abducted, and Isabelle might never see her again.

NINE

Drake was on the phone with the sheriff's office the moment they got Adam back to the cabin. Isabelle tended to his injuries while Drake called in for backup then turned back to Adam for details.

"Did you see the man who took Kelsey?"

He thought for a moment. "Yeah, I saw him. He was tall with big shoulders and dark hair and a mustache. And he had a scar on his cheek. I'm sure it was the same guy that tried to grab her before."

Drake jotted down those details. "Anything else?"

"Only that he was strong. He knocked me away like I was a mosquito. I heard him on the phone with someone as he was dragging Kelsey away. He put her into some kind of hold around her neck and she went limp."

"You saw all of that?" Isabelle asked him.

"Yes, as I was losing consciousness. I wanted to jump up and help her but I just couldn't."

Drake saw the disappointment on Isabelle's face, and Adam must have seen it too.

"I'm sorry, Mrs. Morris. I tried to talk Kelsey into going back to the motel and talking to you."

"I'm sure you did your best," Drake assured him.

"Kelsey's been under a lot of pressure. Any kid would lash out."

"Only not every kid has already had attempts on her life. She should have known better." Isabelle's emotions were wavering between worry and anger. He understood it was sometimes easier to get angry at someone than to face that something terrible might have happened to them.

He put his arm around her. "We'll find her and bring her home. I promise."

She nodded her appreciation and stepped into his arms, pressing her head against his chest. If he could, he would stay that way forever, but their daughter was out there somewhere in danger.

"Adam, do you know how Kelsey called you? Her phone didn't have service."

His face reddened. "She used the hot spot on the motel manager's phone to connect to the internet then texted me. We've been chatting back and forth for the past few days."

Nothing else should have surprised him but that did. They'd all been outsmarted by a fifteen-year-old. He would know better next time...if there was a next time.

"I need to go check in with my team and make a plan," he told Isabelle. She nodded and he turned to Adam. "I'll have a deputy drive you home, Adam."

"I have my car in the public lot."

"Then they'll drive you to it to make certain you get there safely then follow you home. Your parents are waiting there for you. You should call and let them know you're safe. And, if you hear anything from Kelsey, please call the sheriff's office."

"I will."

Drake made arrangements for a patrol deputy to follow the kid home then hurried to where Sheriff Thompson and a group of deputies had set up a command area outside the cabin. When Sheriff Thompson spotted Drake, she updated him on the progress.

"We're setting up a search area and canvassing for witnesses or anyone with cameras in the vicinity. We're also issuing an Amber Alert, so I'll need a photograph of Kelsey."

"I'll get one from Isabelle's cell phone. Adam saw the attacker. Maybe he could work with a sketch artist?" Drake suggested.

She nodded. "That's a good idea. I'll send Pete Richmond over to his house. For now, we'll run with his description of the man. We're also working to track the GPS from Kelsey's phone. We didn't find the device in the initial search so she must still have it on her."

"It won't do any good. Isabelle made her turn it off when they first came to town so no one could find them. I also know Jana double-checked the GPS was off before we returned their phones to them."

"We can contact the phone's carrier and ask if they can turn it on remotely. Jana is already working on that." She saw how concerned he was and put her hand on his shoulder. "We'll find her, Drake." Her eyes glanced over his shoulder, and he turned to see Isabelle standing in the window of the cabin. "I have a feeling we won't have to wait very long before the kidnapper contacts us."

He hadn't considered that. This person had abducted Kelsey as part of the ongoing fight to keep Isabelle from testifying. She would do anything, agree to anything, to protect her daughter, but what was their assurance that the kidnapper would truly return Kelsey if Isabelle cooperated? They couldn't give her back right away—not when Isabelle could go back on her word and testify anyway. So was their plan to hold her until the trial was over? But that could take weeks.

His mind was going in circles trying to figure out this plan. "This doesn't make any sense," he told the sheriff. "What are they planning to do? Hold her until the trial is over?"

Sheriff Thompson didn't look convinced. "I doubt it. I imagine their plan is more permanent than that. You should go and be with Isabelle. Assure her that we're doing everything we can to find her daughter. I'll let you know when we have a solid lead."

He couldn't imagine just sitting around doing nothing and he was sure Isabelle was feeling that too.

He hurried up the porch steps and found her on the couch, her head down. His stomach lurched when he saw that she was typing something into her cell phone, communicating with someone.

"Who are you texting?"

A red flag went up when she slid the phone behind her back and stared up at him guiltily. "No one."

Her face gave her away. He quickly walked over and took the phone from her. The screen displayed a text message from Kelsey's cell phone.

I'll make a trade. You for the girl. She won't be harmed if you give yourself up.

And Isabelle's unsent response.

I'll do anything. Tell me where. Just don't hurt Kelsey.

Dread rolled through him. "What are you doing? Planning to trade yourself for Kelsey?"

She leaped to her feet. "Yes, if that's what it takes to get her back."

"Why didn't you tell me when you received this? I've got the entire Mercy County Sheriff's Office in your front yard and you said nothing? I guess you were just going to try to sneak off too, as Kelsey did? Was that the plan?"

"If necessary. I'll do whatever I have to do to protect my daughter."

"You're forgetting she's my daughter too."

That didn't go over well with her. Her eyes blazed with anger. "How dare you throw that back at me. I've been the one who's been there. I've been the one who's struggled and worked to keep her clothed and fed and out of trouble. I've sacrificed for her."

Her words stung him. They were the truth, but having something that hadn't been his choice thrown back in his face was hurtful. He cared about Kelsey, and losing her would mean losing his last chance to have a relationship with his daughter.

"I might not have the time invested that you have with her but that doesn't mean I'm going to let you do something as reckless and foolish as sacrificing yourself, Izzy."

She grabbed the phone from his hand and quickly hit Send then locked eyes with him. "You don't tell me what to do, Drake. She's my daughter and I'll do what I please."

Anger raced through him. She was going to get both herself and Kelsey killed. He yanked the phone back from her then walked to the door and called to Deputy Gordon, who was closest to the cabin. "Watch her," he instructed

Gordon. "Don't take your eyes off her for even one moment until I get back."

He hurried to the command area and held out the cell phone. "The kidnapper just texted Isabelle. He wants her to trade herself for Kelsey."

Josh picked up the phone and glanced at the screen. He raised an eyebrow, noting her response. "And she said she would."

"Exactly. She will do whatever she has to. I told Gordon to keep an eye on her. We can't leave her alone at all or she'll be gone."

"How?" Sheriff Thompson asked. "She has no car or cell phone so no way to contact the kidnapper."

They'd already been outsmarted by her fifteen-year-old daughter's cleverness. Isabelle was just as smart. Plus, she was desperate. He wasn't going to risk her figuring out a way around him. "I don't want to find out what she might do," he responded. "Hopefully, this guy will text back with a location and we can intercept him. If not, we'll need to see if we can trace this number back to its location and keep Isabelle from doing something foolish at the same time."

He was approaching panic. He'd promised to keep them safe and he'd already had Kelsey abducted under his watch. Now Isabelle wanted to walk into the fire as well. He'd only just got them back. He wasn't losing either one of them.

"We should prepare for both contingencies," Sheriff Thompson stated.

Before she could get started with directions, a text message came through.

There's an old sawmill outside of town. Here are the directions.

He listed the address and Sheriff Thompson quickly responded back.

Where's Kelsey? Is she safe?

She will be. I'll release her once you arrive.

She glanced up at Drake, and he saw she understood as well as he did that if Isabelle arrived for that meeting, neither she nor Kelsey would survive. She sent a return text, still posing as Isabelle.

I'll be there in an hour. Have to sneak past the sheriff's office's team first.

"Josh, put together a team to go set up around the old sawmill."

He nodded. "Will do."

"How did he even know about the sawmill?" Drake wondered. "If he's one of Jeffries's men, wouldn't he be from Memphis? It seems an odd place for an out-of-towner to know."

"Anyone in town could have told him about it. It doesn't matter how he knows, only that he does."

The sheriff's cell phone rang and she scooped it up. "It's Jana." She pressed the answer key then set the phone onto the table. "You're on speaker, Jana. I've got Josh and Drake with me. What did you find? Tell me it's good news."

"I was able to get the cellular carrier to turn on the GPS

data. I've traced the phone to a location near the north side of town at a warehouse. I can't guarantee that's where Kelsey is but that is definitely the location of her phone."

Drake glanced at the address as did Josh, who then asked the question they were all thinking. "So on the other side of town from the old sawmill? Which one do we go to?"

Sheriff Thompson thought for a moment then made the decision. "We have to secure both scenes. We don't yet know if we're dealing with a lone gunman or a group. Every description we've gotten points to this being one man but we can't be certain of that. I'll call the London Sheriff's Office and see if they can provide us with some backup. They're closer to the sawmill so they'll go there. Josh, you take our team to the warehouse."

Josh grabbed a tablet and quickly pulled up an online map of the warehouse. He proceeded to study the area then came up with a plan to breach it. "Okay. We'll treat this mission as if there are multiple assailants. We'll need to pull everyone off the search crews and have them meet up at the sheriff's office to gear up." He turned to Drake. "I'll need you on this. Can you handle it?"

Drake turned and stared back at the cabin. He didn't want to leave Isabelle, but he'd promised to bring Kelsey back.

Josh must have realized the reason for his hesitation. "I wasn't planning on leaving her unprotected. We'll leave Gordon and Sheriff Thompson behind with Isabelle."

He glanced at the sheriff, who nodded and urged him to go. "I'll keep her safe." That reassurance made him feel better.

"Give me a second to speak to Isabelle," he told Josh,

who agreed. As Josh headed up gathering men to join their team, Drake hurried back into the cabin. He walked through the door expecting Isabelle to attack him again, demanding he let her trade herself to the kidnapper. Instead, she stepped into his arms and clung to him, and he could see she'd been crying.

"We know where she is," he told her. "We've located her through her cell phone GPS. She's being held at an old warehouse on the other side of town. My team and I are going to get her and bring her home." She glanced up at him with wet lashes and he kissed her. "I made you a promise, Isabelle, and I intend to keep it. I want us to be a family again. We've already missed too much. I love you and I love Kelsey. I promise I won't let anything happen to her."

She hugged him tightly, and he soaked in the feel of her. This was what he was fighting for. This was what his life had been missing for the past decade.

Before he left, he stopped to talk with Sheriff Thompson. "Please keep her safe."

She smiled and reassured him. "I will. I know you're all very capable, Drake, but I'll be praying for you all regardless. I'll pray you find her safely and bring her home."

He thanked her then walked out. As he climbed into his SUV to head back to the station, he was full of fear at the prospect of losing what he'd only just found.

Lord, please keep them safe.

The Mercy County Sheriff's Office had a good team and he knew all their capabilities. He trusted each and every one of them with his own life. But, did that trust extend beyond himself?

It had to. He had to believe that his daughter's life was in good hands in Mercy's tactical team.

For his part, he was going to do whatever it took to get his family back and keep them both safe.

Drake braced himself for what they might find when they breached the warehouse. No one appeared in sight but they had to be ready for anything. He did his best to calm his racing pulse so he could concentrate on what needed to be done. He'd done tactical missions before with Josh but this time was different. This time, it was his daughter who needed rescuing. And he wasn't going to lose her. Not when he'd only just found her again.

Josh received a text from Sheriff Thompson as they pulled up. "London SO says no one is at the sawmill."

Just as Drake had figured, the abductor was messing with them. Or he might have seen the cops arrive and left. Either way, Drake doubted he'd brought Kelsey with him so he wasn't too concerned. "She's here then," he told Josh, who agreed with his assessment.

Josh parked, but before they got out and set up, he turned to Drake. "Are you sure you want to be a part of this? There's no telling what we might find."

He hadn't told anyone about his true relationship with Kelsey, yet Josh must have realized that Isabelle and Kelsey were important to him. "I'm going in," he told Josh. He hated to think what his daughter was going through, but he had to be there to rescue her. He couldn't bear the thought of losing her now.

Josh didn't argue with him. Instead, he opened the door and climbed out of the truck. Drake did the same and joined the others.

He took his position and waited for Josh to give the signal to breach. At the signal, two other deputies ran at the door with a ramming wedge until it gave. The team poured inside the factory, spreading out to cover all areas. Drake followed behind Josh while the others branched off to check out all the rooms. They searched several areas but came up short. No one seemed to be there.

It didn't make sense that no one was here. They'd tracked the cell phone to this warehouse. Was this just another ruse by the abductors to throw them off? He was filled with a combination of frustration and despair. He couldn't go back to Isabelle without Kelsey. He just couldn't. They had to figure out where she was and fast.

Just as he was about to lose hope, someone called out over the radio. "Here, she's here!"

Drake turned and ran toward the location. He burst into the room to find Kelsey bound and tied to a chair. Deputy Martin was untying her feet as Drake arrived.

"Kelsey!" He ran to her, scooping her up into his arms, and she clung to him, sobs rocking her body. After a moment, he held her at arm's length to check her. "Are you okay? Are you hurt?" He didn't see any life-threatening wounds but he needed to be certain.

She shook her head but tears were in her eyes, and he could see that fear had her rattled. "I'm okay," she assured him. "I'm just so glad you're here. I was so afraid."

He held her and the realization that he'd nearly lost her hit him hard. This was his daughter and he'd come so close to losing her. "I wouldn't let anything happen to you, Kelsey. I promise."

Josh stepped toward them. "All the team has checked

in. The rest of the factory is empty." He looked at Kelsey. "Where is everyone? Why did they leave you here alone?"

Her eyes widened. "What do you mean? You don't have them?"

"No."

Her chin began to quiver. "They didn't want me. They were after my mom. They said they only took me to get to her."

Drake touched her face and tried to reassure her. "I wouldn't let her come. We knew it was a trap."

"No. You don't understand. Leaving her behind was the trap. They knew you would come for me so they deliberately left my cell phone. They heard about the raid over the police radio, so they knew you'd taken the bait, and they left me here to go after Mom."

Dread filled him. They'd been tricked. They'd used Kelsey to get Drake and his team away from the cabin to make it easier to get to Isabelle.

"How many people were there?" he asked Kelsey. "It's important. Try to think."

"I'm not sure. I only saw one man but I thought I heard another person. A woman maybe."

"And they have a police radio," Drake stated. He didn't like the implication of that.

"Or an app or scanner he can listen on," Josh suggested instead. He turned back to Kelsey. "How long have they been gone?" Josh asked her.

She thought for a moment. "Not long. Minutes."

"We still have time," Josh stated.

But Drake knew the truth. "Not much."

Josh pulled out his radio. "I'll call Gordon and Sheriff Thompson to warn them to be on the lookout."

"We have to go now." Drake took Kelsey's arm and led her outside to his SUV. They were at least fifteen minutes away, and who knew how long it had actually been since the attacker had left Kelsey? He prayed it wasn't long.

"When we get there, you stay in the car," he told her. "No matter what, stay in here with the doors locked."

Tears were streaming down her face. "Do you think she's okay?"

"She's going to be fine." The assurances rang hollow even to his own ears.

He switched on his sirens and took off.

The radio squawked. "Gordon is on the lookout. I told him we're on the way," Josh said.

He prayed Gordon could hold off the intruders until they arrived, but he was only one man and they still had no idea how many people were involved. Kelsey had said the assailants listened to a police radio. That meant they probably knew they were on their way now and their time to nab Isabelle was limited.

If they were dealing with a single intruder, that would be better for them, but it still meant Isabelle's life was in danger.

Lord, please keep her safe until I can get to her.

Protection detail was one thing, but Sheriff Thompson was watching Isabelle like a hawk.

Isabelle paced from one end of the cabin to the next, her mind still doing everything it could to figure out a way to get to her daughter. Logically, she knew she needed to wait and let Drake and his team go after Kelsey, but giving up control of her daughter's safety was proving difficult even with Drake.

She'd convinced herself that Drake Shaw was her husband. However, this abduction was really making her question herself. If she truly believed it then she would also have to believe that Drake had as much stake in finding Kelsey and bringing her home as Isabelle did.

She chewed on her nail as she struggled with that concept.

"Drake will find your daughter. He'll bring her home," Sheriff Thompson assured her.

Isabelle knew making that kind of promise could be dangerous. "Should you really be promising that?"

She wanted to believe the sheriff, but the only ones she truly had faith in were Drake...and God.

And she did trust them both. God had been her strength through all the years of raising Kelsey alone and, she was convinced, He'd ultimately brought them here...back to her husband.

Despite the angry words she'd spoken to Drake, she knew he wanted to find Kelsey. Losing her would break his heart. She might never understand what had happened to him that had taken him from her all those years ago, but she was certain her husband had been returned to her. It was time she was thankful for that.

She shrugged as she helped herself to a cup of coffee from the counter. Isabelle had made it earlier just to have something to do. "He's a good man," the sheriff assured her. "One of the finest I've ever known."

She liked hearing her say that about him. The man she'd known had also been a good person, flawed certainly, but with a kind heart. It was one of the traits she saw now in Drake. "How much do you know about Drake and his past?"

"He was thoroughly vetted when he was hired. I've seen his personnel records. He's never spoken much to me about his past, but I'm aware he suffered an injury years ago that left him with some memory loss and that he traveled around a bit before coming to Mercy. I'm happy that he found a home here. We all are."

Only, he'd already had a home he couldn't remember. Isabelle wiped a tear from her cheek then walked into the kitchen. "Let me fix myself a cup of coffee, then I'll fill you in on some details, Sheriff."

"Please call me Deena."

"Deena."

Isabelle poured herself a cup of coffee, and they settled at the kitchen table with a beautiful window overlooking the lake. The view was wasted on her today.

"You and Drake seem to have grown close since you arrived in town. It's obvious to anyone who knows him that he's falling for you."

She felt a little embarrassed that even the sheriff had noticed the attraction between them, but she pressed on. "There's more to the story than you apparently know. That injury you mentioned was an explosion at a refinery where he worked…along with my husband."

"So then they knew one another?"

"Actually, I'm not sure. I don't know all the details and Drake can't remember anything from before the accident. You see, my husband, Rayland, died in that explosion… or so I thought until I came to Mercy."

The realization of what Isabelle was suggesting filled Sheriff Thompson's expression. She set down her cup and leaned forward. "What a minute. Are you saying…?"

Isabelle nodded. "That your Drake Shaw is actually

my husband Rayland Morris? Yes, that's what I believe. I don't know how it happened, and he doesn't know either, but I recognize my husband. It's him."

Sheriff Thompson frowned as she processed this new information. "That's nearly unbelievable. And he had no idea he had a family?"

"I guess not. He thought he was someone else. He was living someone else's life. Unfortunately, his memories of our life together or anything before the explosion have never returned."

"When did you know?"

She thought back to that first moment she'd seen him. "The moment I looked into his eyes. He's spent plenty of time since trying to prove me wrong, but I'm more certain than ever. His sister even admitted she's had her doubts about whether or not she identified the correct man as her brother after the explosion."

"Does that mean he's also Kelsey's father?" Isabelle nodded and she thought about that. "A simple paternity test could confirm his true identity fairly easily. We have a lab in town that could probably have results back in a few hours' time."

Isabelle hadn't considered that but it made sense to compare his DNA with Kelsey's…assuming he brought her home safely.

Sheriff Thompson frowned again. "So I just sent my deputy to rescue his own daughter?" She blew out a breath. "That crafty little schemer. He probably knew I wouldn't have let him go if I'd known the truth about Kelsey. As it was, I confess, I was worried about him going on the mission given how close you've become, but this… I had no idea."

Isabelle didn't mean to get him into trouble. "I think he's just confused about everything. He seems to know the truth but just hasn't processed it yet."

"He's been too consumed with keeping you both safe."

Her radio cackled and she spoke into the mic. "What is it, Gordon?"

"Sheriff, I think someone's approach—" Before he could finish, a loud commotion sounded then they heard Gordon grunt before the line went dead.

Sheriff Thompson's other hand went to her weapon and she stood, instantly on alert. Isabelle stood too and moved closer to the sheriff, who motioned for her to stand away from the front door.

She pressed the button on the radio. "Gordon, report." She waited only a moment with no response before she pulled her gun from its holster and walked to the door. "Stay inside and lock this behind me."

She pulled open the door then raised her gun as she scanned the surroundings. The sheriff motioned for Isabelle to close the door and she did so, turning the lock then looking around for something to grab to use as a weapon in case of a fight. She landed on a poker from the fireplace set. It was iron and heavy. She grabbed it and held it up, prepared to defend herself if needed.

It was eerily quiet outside, and she wished for some way to communicate with the sheriff. She pulled out her cell phone, hoping for a call from Drake saying they'd gotten Kelsey, but there was nothing.

Too much time passed with no indication that the sheriff had given the all clear. Isabelle jumped at every noise but moved toward the door, poker raised and ready to fight.

Suddenly, gunshots rang from outside. Isabelle jumped with fright at the sound and what it meant. She moved to the window and pulled back the curtain, glancing outside, but she saw no movement anywhere.

She called out for the sheriff then for Gordon, only neither answered her.

She pulled out her cell phone and pressed the button to dial Drake. Only, before she could press send on the call, gunfire hit the front door and it burst open. A large figure stood in the doorway.

Isabelle screamed and turned to run, her cell phone slipping from her hand. There was no time to stop and retrieve it as the man who entered raised his gun to fire. Shots rang out as she darted up the stairs and into her bedroom.

She heard his footsteps on the stairs and knew she had very little time. The window was a second-floor jump, and she wasn't sure she could make it through the window before he found her.

She had no choice but to hide.

The closet was standing open so she ducked inside it and huddled in a corner, the poker still in her hand ready to use as a means of defense.

She heard the intruder's heavy steps as he went to the room across the hallway first then checked the bathroom. Isabelle's heart was racing with fear, and she began to wonder if she could make it past him and back downstairs to grab her cell phone before he entered this room.

She'd just about decided to try when she heard the door open. She leaned back as far as she could into the corner, even as she knew she wouldn't be hard to find. There weren't that many places to hide.

Her mind spun wondering what had happened to the sheriff and Deputy Gordon. It must be bad if they hadn't come to help. Had this man harmed them? Were they even still alive? She could only hope and pray that they were okay—and that one or both of them, or Drake, would show up before this man found her.

He stopped in front of the closet, and Isabelle could see his outline. Fear raced through her as he hesitated then seemed to walk away. She nearly cried out in relief, but it was short-lived.

A cell phone rang, and she could see him digging for it. "Yeah?" He'd obviously placed the call on speaker because a woman's voice came through loud and clear.

"Simon, why haven't you answered my calls? I've been trying to reach you."

Isabelle lifted her hand to her mouth in shock, barely managing to keep herself from crying out at hearing the woman. She recognized the voice right away.

Tracy.

Why would Tracy be calling the man trying to kill Isabelle?

"I was a little busy," he told her. "I had to wait until they arrived at the warehouse to find the girl before I headed to the cabin. Then I had to take out two cops."

"Well? Is it done?"

Isabelle's heart plummeted at the simple question. Had her best friend really just asked if Simon had killed her yet? She pressed her hand to her mouth to keep from crying out.

"Not yet. She's hiding but I'll find her."

Hot tears pressed against her eyes and a few slipped through. She had to force herself to not sob at the realization of Tracy's betrayal. It was bad enough her life was in danger, but to know her best friend was responsible was more than she could handle.

She was trying to process this new information when the closet doors were flung open and the man grabbed her arm. She hadn't even realized he'd ended his call and had started searching for her again. Self-preservation quickly pushed its way past the fear and betrayal, and she gripped the iron poker tighter as the man Tracy had called Simon yanked her from her hiding spot.

She came out swinging, slamming the iron poker. He cried out in pain and blood poured from the wound she'd caused. He cursed and grabbed his head, and Isabelle slipped from his grasp and took off running.

He growled then shouted at her. "Get back here!"

She didn't stop running until she hit the bottom step. Her cell phone had slipped from her hand somewhere near the base of the steps but she didn't see it anywhere. It must have slid beneath something. As badly as she wanted to find it, she knew she didn't have time to search. He was already stumbling down the stairs, grumbling as he descended them.

She ran to the kitchen and searched for something she could use to defend herself. She still had the poker, but although it was heavy, it wasn't sharp enough to do any real damage. And she doubted she would get another opportunity to swing it at him. He would be better prepared for it next time.

She dropped the poker and reached for a sharp knife instead. Feeling a little better now that she was better armed, she decided that she had to get out of the cabin and find help. Without being able to call anyone, it was her best option. If she could find Sheriff Thompson or Deputy Gordon that would be best, but even if something had happened to them, their vehicles were parked out front. She could use the radio to alert Drake and others that they needed help.

But, first, she needed to get to the door.

She didn't hear Simon moving around, but she knew he hadn't left. She peeked through the kitchen doorway and glanced around, noticing a trail of blood leading from the stairs. Probably he'd gone in search of a towel or something to stop the bleeding. The door was only one mad dash away. She had to risk it.

Only, she didn't make it far before she heard his voice. "You're not going anywhere, lady," the man said, stepping out from behind a corner as she headed for the door. He pulled her against him and hit her hard in the face. "I'll teach you to hit me in the head with a fireplace poker." She hit the floor and the knife skittered away as pain radiated through her cheek and jaw. Once she was able to catch her breath, she eyed the knife. She needed to reach it. Escape was still her best choice, but if she couldn't get away from him, she would have to fight.

She scrambled for the knife, but he laughed at her attempt and kicked her hard in the side before she could reach it.

Pain blinded her and all she could do was gasp for breath.

But she wasn't giving up. She tried again, army crawling toward her only hope for survival.

He approached her again, this time bending over to grab her shoulders. She saw her opportunity and fought through the agony to reach for the knife. Her fingertips touched the handle and then it was in her hand.

He spun her over, his face registering shock at the sight of the weapon she was holding. The shock deepened even further when she stabbed it into his chest with all the force she could muster.

He stumbled backward. She'd managed to hit a soft spot and the knife had plunged deep. She had no idea how injured he was, but as he fell to his knees, she scrambled to her feet and ran for the door.

Gunfire startled her then something stung her, sending her falling back to the floor. Her hand went to the side of her stomach where the pain was the worst, and when she pulled it back up to look at it, it came back bloody. She turned and saw that while Simon had gone down, he'd managed to pull his gun and shoot her first. He hit the floor hard and the gun skittered away. It didn't seem possible that he'd be getting up again but she couldn't take that risk. She needed to reach the gun.

Only the pain was excruciating and trying to get up again sent her head spinning. With every moment that passed, moving became more difficult. She tried to fight off the fog of pain and exhaustion that was urging her to close her eyes. She couldn't give in. She needed to get to help. She needed to find Drake and Kelsey.

Kelsey. He'd admitted on the phone to taking out Sheriff Thompson and Deputy Gordon but he hadn't said if he'd hurt her daughter. He'd come to town to kill Isabelle, and if help didn't arrive soon, she had a feeling he was going to succeed in his mission after all, but that wasn't what truly mattered to her. The tears came again, this time at not knowing whether her daughter was dead or alive. Where was Drake and why hadn't he let her know Kelsey was safe? Was it because she wasn't and he didn't know how to tell her? Or had Simon ambushed them at the warehouse before coming to the cabin? A different kind of pain filled her at the thought of losing Drake and Kelsey, and tears slipped down the side of her face.

She didn't know if they were alive, and, now, she might never know.

Her strength was fading and she felt the life draining from her body. She could see Simon, who still hadn't moved. He was dead…and Isabelle was sure to be close behind him.

Tracy and Charles Jeffries had taken everything from her. She knew why Jeffries wanted her dead, but why had Tracy done this to her?

What she wouldn't give for one more opportunity to tell Drake she loved him or to hold Kelsey. There were so many regrets. If she'd only given Rayland the second chance he'd asked for in their marriage, none of this would have happened. They wouldn't have spent the last ten years apart.

Yet, she was thankful for the time God had returned him to her, brief as it had been.

Images of her daughter laughing and squealing with delight as her father pushed her on the swing set, just like in the images he'd drawn, filled her head and her heart. It was a wonderful memory that hadn't been completely stolen from him in the explosion. They'd been so happy once upon a time, and they should have been again.

Darkness played around the edges of her vision and all the strength left her body. It felt like she was floating away and had one last silent plea to God as the darkness pulled her under.

Jesus, please take care of my family.

TEN

Drake screeched to a halt in front of the cabin and threw open the driver's door. "Stay here," he told Kelsey. He didn't see Gordon and that immediately struck him as wrong. He should have been patrolling or standing guard by the door.

And neither he nor Sheriff Thompson had answered their calls.

As he approached the cabin, he noted the door stood partly open. Bullet holes on it caused him to reach for his weapon. Moments later, he heard the pop of gunfire, which propelled Drake into the cabin. He shouted once again at Kelsey, who'd opened the door of the SUV at the sound. "Stay there!"

He pushed open the door and his heart fell. Isabelle was lying unmoving on the floor and blood was pooling around her. A man he recognized from the sketch Adam had given them lay several feet away. He didn't appear to be moving either.

Drake rushed over to him. Seeing the gun a foot or so away, he kicked it farther so that even if the man managed to rouse himself, he couldn't grab it. Not that that seemed likely. He checked the man's pulse—and, as expected, he found nothing. He was dead and the obvious knife sticking out from his chest was most likely the cause.

Isabelle had fought back, but as he looked over at her, he could see that the assailant had gotten off a shot at her.

He glanced around. Kelsey had mentioned hearing a woman's voice but a quick scan of the kitchen and living room showed no one else. He needed to clear the rest of the house and search for Gordon and Sheriff Thompson, but first he needed to check on Isabelle.

She hadn't reacted at all when he'd entered and hadn't moved.

He hurried to her, unsettled by how still she was and the pallor of her skin. Only her low moaning told him she was still alive and he was thankful for that. He rushed into the kitchen for towels and pressed them against her stomach wound, which looked bad. She needed help and she needed it now.

He heard more noises from outside and what sounded like vehicles and car doors. Josh and the rest of the team. Finally. He'd rushed ahead of them at the thought of Isabelle being in danger. "I need an ambulance," he called out. He'd left his radio in the SUV with Kelsey but he heard the rapid pace of footsteps and knew someone was approaching.

Josh hurried inside, gun raised as he surveyed the scene.

"The gunman's dead but Isabelle needs an ambulance now," Drake explained. "I haven't cleared the rest of the house to see if there's any other perpetrators."

Josh quickly made the call for an ambulance as he hurried over to check on her. He pressed his finger to her wrist and Drake saw a hint of relief on his face. Yes, she was still alive but she wouldn't be for long if help didn't arrive fast. The towel he was using was already soaking through. The injury was serious—maybe even critical.

"Gordon and Sheriff Thompson weren't here when I arrived," Drake told him.

"They must be here somewhere." Josh stood and hurried outside, all the while calling out for help on the radio.

Drake knew he should go help him find out what had happened to their friends, but he couldn't bear to leave Isabelle. He prayed they were safe but this was his main concern at the moment, at least until the ambulance arrived.

Lord, please let that be soon.

He didn't like how Isabelle struggled to breathe. It caused him to struggle too. He couldn't lose her now, not when he finally had a chance to be a family with Isabelle and with Kelsey.

He sat on the floor and positioned himself so that her head was in his lap. He knew you weren't supposed to move injured victims, but if these were their last moments together, he wanted to touch her and be near her so she wouldn't feel alone. He leaned down and kissed her cheek then whispered, "I love you, Izzy," in her ear.

Her eyelids fluttered then opened partway. "Kelsey?"

"She's fine. She's outside," Drake assured her.

She seemed to be struggling to reach up her hand and touch his face so he took it and held it to his cheek. Her voice was weak and drained but her stubbornness shone through too as she insisted on getting out her words. "Promise me that you'll take care of her, Ray. Promise you'll be there for her."

"I will. We'll both be there for her, Izzy. She needs us both. You're going to be fine."

"Ray—"

"I'm not going to lose you again, Izzy." He pressed his face into her hand. "I can't. You hold on. Help is on the way."

"I love you, Ray."

He stroked her cheek. "I love you too and I'm not letting you go. I just got you and Kelsey back. I won't lose you again."

That seemed to settle her—maybe too much so, because her arm went limp in his hand. Her eyes fluttered again then closed, and he feared he'd lost her even as he heard her gurgling for breath.

"Mama!" Kelsey burst into the front door and ran to them. She threw herself to the floor, tears streaming down her face. She looked to be bordering on hysterical. He could see the horror and guilt in her expression—and while he understood where her feelings were coming from, he knew he needed to keep her grounded too. He gave her a task.

Drake tossed her a towel. "Press it hard against her wound to try to stop the bleeding."

She stared at Drake with fear in her young, wide and wet eyes. "Is she going to die?" Her voice cracked with anguish, and Drake wanted to reassure her that Isabelle was going to be okay...but he wasn't sure she would be.

"We'll get through this," he told her instead.

No matter what happened, he still had Kelsey to look after.

He heard the sounds of the ambulance arriving and two paramedics rushed inside. "She's got a gunshot wound to the abdomen. She's been in and out of consciousness and she's struggling to breathe," he told them.

"How long ago was she shot?" one of them asked, glancing at the blood loss evidence on the towels and hardwood.

It seemed like hours since he'd burst in and found her. "Minutes ago. Maybe five."

The paramedic glanced at Kelsey and Drake. "I'm going to have to ask you to move away and make room so we can work," he stated.

Drake stood but Kelsey clung to Isabelle, paralyzed by fear and grief. Drake took her arm and pulled her away. "Let these men work," he told her, understanding that she was blocking their access to Isabelle.

Drake placed his hand on her arm and helped her stand. She fell right into his arms and he held her. They needed each other now.

A different paramedic walked to the shooter and checked on him. Drake turned Kelsey away from that scene, unsure if she'd even noticed the man. He didn't relish the sight of someone losing their life, but this man had come here to kill and paid the price.

If only Drake had been just a few moments earlier.

Josh walked back into the cabin and moved toward him. Drake wasn't sure he could drag Kelsey outside and he didn't want to leave her either. He braced himself for Josh's update on the sheriff and Gordon, praying it was good news.

"We found both Sheriff Thompson and Gordon. They were both shot and stuffed into the back of Gordon's patrol car. Thankfully, they were both wearing vests so they weren't seriously hurt. They're alive and okay."

He breathed a sigh of relief at that. At last, some good news.

Josh glanced down at Isabelle as the paramedics worked

frantically to find a vein for an IV and assess her wounds. He patted Drake's shoulder. "I'm praying for her. We all are."

Another paramedic arrived with a gurney, and Drake watched as four of them loaded Isabelle onto it then wheeled her outside to the waiting ambulance. Drake held Kelsey's hand as they followed it, watching as they loaded her inside and closed the doors.

Kelsey sniffed back tears. "She looked so bad."

"She's still breathing," he said. "That's a good thing. She's a fighter, isn't she?"

She nodded then let out a chuckle as she wiped her face. "She's super stubborn."

Yes, she was. She was the one who wouldn't take no for an answer when he'd insisted he wasn't Rayland. She was the one who hadn't let the question of his identity go. And he was glad now that she hadn't.

He pulled Kelsey to him and she clung to him. If the worst did happen, if they lost Isabelle, Kelsey would need him more than ever. But that wasn't what he wanted. He wanted them to be a family again.

He glanced at another ambulance to see Sheriff Thompson and Gordon being treated for their injuries. He was glad they were okay. It was bad enough that Isabelle was fighting for her life. He couldn't bear to lose anyone else he cared for.

As the ambulance roared away, he led Kelsey back to his SUV. "Let's go. We'll follow the ambulance to the hospital."

Lord, we need You.

It seemed too cruel to finally find his family only to lose them again.

* * *

Drake's leg bobbed up and down nervously as they waited for news of Isabelle. She'd been taken straight to surgery when she'd arrived at the hospital, but they had yet to hear how she was.

Kelsey stayed close to him and even laid her head on his shoulder as the minutes turned into hours. He wanted to broach the subject of his true identity, but he didn't feel the moment was right to break the news.

The waiting room began to fill as people from the sheriff's office and around town arrived to sit with them and pray. Sheriff Thompson was an especially welcomed entry, and Drake stood when she arrived. Her hair was loose around her shoulders in a casual manner and she was wearing a pair of hospital scrubs.

"How are you?" he asked her.

"I'm okay. Gordon and I are both okay. He's got a bullet wound in his shoulder but he's going to be fine. He said he'll call to check in on you later once the doctors are finished with him." The irony of Gordon calling to check on him when he'd been injured struck Drake as funny, but he couldn't bring himself to laugh. He glanced around the waiting area and saw people from his church, neighbors who'd heard about the incident, and several members of the Mercy County Sheriff's Office staff and deputies, including Josh, Jana, Sabrina and her husband, Jake, all stopping in to offer their prayers and support.

It made him feel good that so many people cared about them.

"Kelsey!"

Drake turned to see Adam enter the waiting area. Following behind him were his parents.

He glanced at Kelsey, whose face lit up at seeing him. She leaped from her chair and ran to him. "Oh, Adam."

He quickly pulled her into a hug. "I was so worried. I'm sorry. I shouldn't have come with you. I should have told you to stay at the motel, where it was safe."

She glanced around guiltily. "I shouldn't have sneaked away. I was just so angry. I messed everything up. I'm sorry you got hurt."

The teens moved to a corner to sit and chat and Mrs. Burch turned to Drake. "Did you catch the man who did this?"

He nodded. "He won't be bothering anyone again."

"Has there been any word on Kelsey's mother's condition? We never met her, but Adam's had nothing but good things to say about her and Kelsey."

Drake pulled a hand down his face as he shook his head. "Not yet. We're still waiting."

"Is it okay if we stay for a while? Adam was so worried about Kelsey and insisted we bring him, but if we're in the way, we'll go."

"No, please, of course you're welcome to stay. In fact, I'm glad you're here. Adam's been a good friend to Kelsey."

She smiled. "I'll say. He's definitely smitten with her."

As they moved away to sit with their son, Sheriff Thompson took Drake's arm and pulled him aside. "This might not be the right time to bring this up but I wanted you to know that Isabelle told me about your unusual situation."

"She did?" It seemed odd that they'd had that conversation, but he was glad to know he didn't have to explain.

"Whenever you're ready, we can perform a simple paternity test. We'll get a sample from both you and Kelsey. If it shows you're her father then you'll know for certain who you really are. If you're not then at least you'll have the answers you've been seeking."

He'd never thought about a paternity test, but it was a simple method to settle things, and he knew that the tests were extremely accurate. He turned to look at Kelsey soberly trying hard not to smile at something Adam said. They would do the test when the time was right, but in his heart, he realized that he didn't need a test to know the truth. He knew with every fiber of his being who he was.

He thanked her then chatted a few minutes with his pastor and his wife, but his mind was always on the clock as the hours ticked away.

Finally, the doors to the operating room opened. The doctor stepped out and glanced around the room. "Who is the family of Isabelle Morris?"

Drake beelined for him and so did Kelsey.

"Are you her husband?" he asked.

He didn't hesitate to answer. "I am."

"Isabelle is going to be fine. We were able to remove the bullet and repair the damage it did. She'll make a full recovery."

The room erupted in happiness. Relief flooded him and he pulled Kelsey to him. "Thank you, Jesus," Drake whispered and heard Kelsey respond with her own, "Amen."

"She'll be sleeping for a while, but you're welcome to go in and sit with her once she's in a room. A nurse will let you know when it's time."

He thanked the doctor then hugged Kelsey again. It was only at that moment that he realized the girl hadn't flinched when he'd claimed to be Isabelle's husband.

It was time to tell her everything.

"Kelsey, when the doctor asked if I was Isabelle's husband and I said I was—"

She halted his explanation. "It's okay. I already know."

He was surprised by how calm she seemed. "You already know what exactly?"

"I overheard you and mom talking. She thinks you're her husband and my father. She thought you were dead but you just lost your memory. It's like a Lifetime movie or a Harlequin romance novel."

He rubbed his chin as he digested her words. She did indeed know everything. Only, he couldn't gauge how she felt about learning her father might be alive. "And what do you think about that?"

She shrugged. "Mom's usually right."

That made him smile. "I suppose you would know that better than me but I tend to agree. There's a test you and I can take to confirm it. Whenever you're ready, it's just a mouth swab. But, Kelsey, if it comes back that it's true, that I am your father, I owe you for all the years I wasn't there for you."

"Are you kidding me? You kept us safe and you rescued me from a kidnapper. You've got nothing to make up for." She gave him another quick hug then changed gears. "Can I go back and sit with Adam until Mom wakes up?"

"Sure, go ahead."

He was amazed at how mature she seemed in one moment then how innocent the next. He'd missed his chance to watch her grow up but he had years to get to know her again. He couldn't wait.

A nurse approached him. "Mrs. Morris is back in a room now. You and your daughter can see her now."

He thanked her and motioned Kelsey over. As he did, he realized how full this room was with all the people in his life.

The people of Mercy.

His family.

He'd been feeling alone for so long thinking he didn't belong anywhere, when the truth was that God had brought him to Mercy, to an extended family, one he was especially thankful for in this moment.

It was one he was looking forward to adding Isabelle and Kelsey to.

Pain was the first sensation Isabelle felt as she fought to open her eyes. She glanced around to see she was in a hospital bed with IVs and wires hooked up to her. She tried to move but her body protested and she groaned out in pain.

"Careful, or you'll pull out your IV again."

She glanced over to see Drake sitting in the chair beside the bed. A smile spread across his face. "Good morning."

"Is it morning?"

He glanced at his watch then shook his head. "Not really. How do you feel?"

"Like I've been shot and left for dead." She tried to make light of it, but Drake frowned instead of smiling.

"Don't joke about it, Izzy. We nearly lost you. We came way too close."

The fogginess of her brain began to fade and so did a rush of memories. The assassin. Being shot and very nearly dying. Drake's voice whispering he loved her.

Then another memory surfaced. Her daughter being abducted. "Kelsey! Is she okay?"

"She's fine. She's safe. He didn't hurt her. Taking Kelsey was just a lure to get you alone. She's waiting out in the waiting room. They'll only allow one of us to stay with you so we've been alternating sitting with you. I just relieved her an hour ago."

"How long have I been out?"

"Eight hours."

The last thing she really remembered clearly was the assassin bursting into the cabin and fighting him off. But the reason she'd been alone in the cabin...it was because Sheriff Thompson had gone outside to find out why Gordon hadn't responded. "Sheriff Thompson, Gordon, are they both okay?"

"They're both fine. They were both shot but they were wearing bulletproof vests, so neither was seriously hurt. They've both been by checking in on you."

She was thankful for that at least given the betrayal she'd suffered. "What about the gunman?"

He was quick to reassure her. "He's dead. You'll have to explain to me how he shot you yet you killed him."

She was glad the threats against her were over. Only, they weren't completely over yet, were they? The sting of her friend's betrayal still loomed over her. "He was only a hired gun. I heard a phone call between him and my supposed best friend, Tracy Goode. She hired that man, Simon, to kill me to keep me from testifying."

He frowned. "Kelsey did mention she thought she'd heard a woman's voice at the warehouse, only we didn't find anyone else there or at the cabin."

"I overheard her on the phone with him—he listened

to the call on speakerphone. She's probably still back in Memphis."

He nodded. "We can alert the local police to get eyes on her and take her into custody."

"What about Jeffries? He must have been involved too, right?"

"We're not sure yet, but if he was, he didn't get what he wanted. Sheriff Thompson has been on the phone with the prosecutor. She was able to get your testimony pushed back to a later date so it can wait until you're strong enough to testify."

That was good. She'd nearly died to cover up her boss's fraud. She wasn't about to back down now when he needed to be in prison.

Drake took her hand and held it. "I'm sorry I didn't make it back to you in time. It looks like he used Kelsey to lure us away from you. You were always his primary target."

"I know. Kelsey must have been so frightened."

"She's strong. Like her mother."

"And she's really okay, Drake?"

"Yes, she's fine except for being worried about you. Adam's parents brought him by when you first arrived here to comfort Kelsey. They just dropped him back off a while ago. He's sitting out there with her waiting for you to wake up."

She was glad Adam had been there for Kelsey. This entire ordeal would certainly have been more difficult for her daughter without her new friend. "He's a good kid."

"Yes, he is. He'll be heartbroken without her when she heads back to Memphis. Apparently, there's this dance at school in a few weeks he was hoping to take her to."

"Well, he won't have to be without her. Kelsey and I aren't planning to go anywhere."

His face lit up with a smile. "Yeah?"

"In case you hadn't noticed, I'm currently unemployed. And, after what we've been through, I can't imagine returning to Memphis. The way my so-called friends turned on me when they learned about my role in the case was devastating. I know Kelsey will miss her friends but she's made connections here too."

"Does that mean you're staying in Mercy?" The hopefulness in his expression warmed her. He wanted her here and this was the place she wanted to be.

"Yes, we are."

He leaped to his feet and planted a kiss on her. "I'll go get Kelsey. She'll want to know you're awake, and you can tell her the good news."

She grabbed his arm as he started to move away. As much as she wanted to see her daughter, she didn't want Drake to leave her side either. "Wait, don't go yet."

He sat back down and covered her hand still on his arm. "What is it?"

"Back at the cabin when I thought it was the end for me, you said you loved me. Did you mean that?"

His eyes widened then he smiled. "Absolutely, I did. I love you, Isabelle. I can't remember a time when I didn't love you. Only…"

Her heart skipped a beat as he hesitated.

His face grew serious. "You called me Ray. When you were in anguish, you called out his name. I know that I am him. Even my sister admitted it was possible. But I'm not sure I know how to be Rayland. I have no memory of being him."

"That doesn't matter to me. I'm not the same person I was back then either. I want us to get to know each other all over again, as who we are now. And I don't care what name you go by as long as I can call you my husband." She touched his cheek, and he smiled and leaned into her hand.

"I've searched for so long to find out where I belong," he told her. "Now, I know. I belong with you and Kelsey. The only place I want to be is by your side. Will you marry me…again?"

She smiled as her heart warmed and she pulled him to her for a kiss. "There's nothing I want more."

He reluctantly pulled away from her. "I'd better go let Kelsey know you're awake."

"Tell her I want to see her. I want to let her know that we're going to be a family again."

As he went to share the news with their daughter, Isabelle's heart overflowed. Somehow, she'd been given a second chance at love, a second chance to make different decisions, and she intended to cherish it. God had truly restored all that she had lost.

Thank You, Jesus.

The door to her room opened again moments after he'd left and a nurse walked in. The fact that she was wearing a mask didn't immediately strike Isabelle as odd. However, as she moved closer, Isabelle's guard went up as she recognized the eyes of her former friend.

Tracy!

Isabelle stiffened and raced to find the call button, but Tracy was faster. She grabbed it and pulled it out of reach.

Isabelle did her best to sit up and locked eyes with her friend. "What's your plan here, Tracy?"

She pulled the mask down and pasted on a friendly smile. "What do you mean? I was just seeing how you are, Isabelle. I heard what happened to you."

"You mean that you came to see if I was dead?"

Her friend's expression hardened. "What?"

"I overheard you on the phone with Simon. You hired that man to kill me, Tracy. I want to know why. How could you do that? I thought we were friends."

This time, her expression twisted and she smirked. "We were, Isabelle, at least until you turned against Charles."

Now confusion mixed in with the fear and pain surging through her. "I don't understand."

"I'm in love with Charles Jeffries, and you're trying to send him to prison for the rest of his life. I can't allow that to happen."

Her sorry excuse for trying to kill them changed Isabelle's fear to anger. "So you threatened my daughter? You threatened my life over a man?"

"You're the one who put your daughter in danger, Isabelle. Don't blame me for your recklessness."

She couldn't believe her friend could do something like that, but she'd heard it with her own ears. "Does Jeffries know what you did? Was he involved?"

"You're always trying to find something to blame him for, Isabelle. He's not the monster you're making him out to be."

"He hurt innocent people. He stole people's life savings and left them destitute."

"It's their own fault for not being smarter. You can't blame Charles because people made bad decisions financially."

"You can when he was the one who stole their money."

Tracy sighed and waved away Isabelle's argument. "You're always trying to make something out of nothing."

Her friend was unbelievable. Clearly, there was no reasoning with her. She didn't care about anyone but herself. "Simon is dead in case you didn't know. And the police have been alerted that you were involved. They're probably raiding your apartment as we speak."

"Good thing I'm not there."

"So what's your plan now, Tracy? Did you come here to finish what Simon couldn't? Are you going to kill me yourself?"

She pulled a knife from her back pocket and shrugged. "As a matter of fact, I am. I'm sorry it came to this, but I have to do what I have to do. You shouldn't have stuck your nose where it didn't belong."

She raised the knife and lunged at Isabelle, who rolled from the bed and hit the floor, all the cords attached to her pulling out. The alarms from the machines started going off as she crawled to the bedside table. If she could reach the phone, she could call for help.

Tracy grabbed her before she could make it to the phone and dragged her away as she raised the knife over her head again. Isabelle grabbed her arm and held it, struggling to keep her from plunging it into her. She held Tracy off for several moments but could feel herself weakening. It looked like she wasn't going to have that happy ending after all.

Suddenly, the door opened and Drake and Kelsey burst into the room. Kelsey screamed, causing Tracy to turn, knife still in hand.

Drake pulled his gun and aimed it at her. "Put it down," he ordered her.

She thought for a moment then raised it again.

He fired and Tracy collapsed beside Isabelle. The knife fell from her hand as she clutched her shoulder.

Drake hurried to her and kicked it away from her grasp. "Don't move," he warned her, keeping his gun trained on her.

Suddenly, the room filled with people, including hospital security and nurses. Several nurses hurried to Isabelle while others rushed to treat Tracy's wound. "Once they've treated her, a deputy will be taking her into custody for kidnapping and attempted murder. Make sure she's secure," Drake instructed the security officers about Tracy.

He knelt beside Isabelle. "Are you okay? Did she hurt you?"

She shook her head. "She wanted to but she didn't get the chance." She touched his cheek. "You came just in time."

She was quick to assure Kelsey that she was okay, as Tracy was escorted out of the room to be treated then arrested. Drake lifted her in his arms and placed her back onto the bed.

Kelsey was still struggling to make sense of what had just happened. "Is it true, Mama? Did Tracy really try to kill you?"

Tracy had always seemed to be a good friend and had shown Kelsey a lot of attention. She'd betrayed not only Isabelle but her too. "It's true, Kelsey. She hired the man who was after us. I heard her talking to him. She was the one behind everything."

"But I thought it was your boss who was behind this."

"We think he still is but he can't hurt us anymore."

"There will be an armed guard at your door from now on," Drake assured her. "No one is going to harm either one of you ever again, not as long as I'm around."

She took both his and Kelsey's hands, overcome with happiness despite another close call. Her daughter was here and Drake was back in her life again. Her family had finally been restored to her and nothing would separate them again.

She turned to her daughter to share the good news about Drake asking her to marry him. "Honey, there's something you should know."

Kelsey held up her hands. "I already know. He's my dad and not dead as you previously thought. I'm all caught up."

Surprised, Isabelle looked at Drake, who shrugged. "I was going to tell her too but she already knew. She overheard us talking and she actually seems okay with it."

Isabelle turned back to Kelsey, who nodded. "It might be nice to have a dad again."

That was good to hear. "I hope you're also okay with us getting married too because Drake asked me to marry him and I said yes."

"Congratulations!" Kelsey hugged Isabelle but still had questions. "What does that mean? Is he moving back to Memphis with us?"

Kelsey's look of anticipation said it all. She was hoping the opposite would be true. Isabelle quickly put her daughter out of her misery. "No, honey, we're staying in Mercy."

She squealed with delight then hugged them both before proclaiming, "I need to go tell Adam the good news." She bounded from the room.

"I guess that's the seal of approval," she told Drake, who nodded.

"You're going to love Mercy."

She smiled and leaned into him. "I already do."

She was home again.

EPILOGUE

Isabelle bounded down the steps of the courthouse stairs with Drake on her heels. She was filled with elation and satisfaction at the guilty verdict that had just been handed down for Charles Jeffries on multiple counts of fraud and embezzlement.

A crowd of reporters gathered as the prosecutor descended the steps to discuss the conviction. Thankfully, they were able to push Isabelle's testimony to the end of the trial while Isabelle recovered from her gunshot wounds. She'd returned to Memphis to testify and had played her role in bringing down Jeffries, just as she'd committed to do. Now, two months later, she and Drake had returned to hear the jury's verdict.

It was an easy decision to come. They were in town packing up her and Kelsey's house that had recently been sold. They were remaining in Mercy permanently. Kelsey had enrolled in the high school there and was thriving with her new friends. She'd remained behind in Mercy, staying with Sheriff Thompson while Isabelle and Drake were away, in order to attend the fall dance with Adam.

Drake stood behind her, wrapping his arms around her waist and settling his chin on her shoulder, as they watched the press toss question after question. Charles Jeffries would remain in prison on appeal given the new charges the district attorney was filing against him in Mercy for conspiracy to commit kidnapping and attempted murder. Tracy was also in jail awaiting trial on the same charges. So far, she'd refused to implicate Jeffries in her plans to hire a hitman to kill Isabelle, but the district attorney believed he had enough evidence to indict him anyway. Isabelle was happy to leave this part of her life behind her once and for all and begin again with her family in Mercy.

The paternity test had shown Drake was indeed Kelsey's father, which proved he'd been misidentified. He was Rayland Morris. And, although his sister had been devastated at learning her error and its consequences, Isabelle held no ill will toward her. She'd done the best she could at the time. She'd met her and hoped to form a closer bond between both families who'd lost so much that tragic day ten years earlier.

"I have an idea," Drake whispered in her ear.

She turned to him, curious at his playful tone. "What do you have in mind?"

"Well, we are at the courthouse and there's no waiting period in Tennessee. What do you say we apply for a license then find a judge who'll marry us today?"

The excitement in his manner thrilled her. Since discovering his real identity, there had been a lot of discussions about what to call him and what needed to be done. He'd decided to continue to use the name Drake Shaw since it was the name of the man he was now and all he remembered, but they'd put off marriage until the legal stuff was sorted out. However, they'd been unprepared for the amount of paperwork and legal red tape necessary to reclaim his identity. Technically, she was still married to Rayland, but, also technically, he was legally dead. They'd found themselves in a web of bureaucracy that had prevented them from moving forward.

"That's an amazing idea but who am I marrying? Drake or Ray?"

He put his hands over her face and pulled her close. "It doesn't matter. We're both in love with you," he told her before kissing her long and deep.

That was good enough for her.

As they hurried back up the steps to find a judge, Isabelle texted Kelsey the news. She would have liked to have had Kelsey at the ceremony, but she also didn't want to wait another day to be married. She hoped her daughter would understand.

Finally, was Kelsey's reply along with a heart emoji.

Isabelle shared that feeling, happy her daughter didn't feel excluded. Finally, she was whole again.

* * * * *

If you enjoyed this book in Virginia Vaughan's
Lone Star Defenders miniseries,
be sure to read these previous titles:

Dangerous Christmas Investigation
Missing in Texas

Available from Love Inspired Suspense!

Dear Reader,

We're smack-dab in the middle of this new series, and so far, I'm loving these characters. I hope you are too.

This story means so much to me because it touches on the theme of second chances. It's also a back from the dead story, which is one of my favorite tropes. How often do we look at our circumstances and believe all hope is lost? We forget that we worship the maker of the world! I regularly have to remind myself that, if God can create the world from nothing, He can certainly handle my messes. And He can!

Join me as I continue through this new series and get to know these Lone Star Defenders. I'm looking forward to diving into Sheriff Deena Thompson's story up next. I can't wait to share it with you!

I love hearing from my readers. You can reach me online through my website www.virginiavaughanonline.com or on Facebook at www.facebook.com/ginvaughanbooks. You can also reach out to me through the publisher.

Blessings and happy reading!
Virginia